SECRET AGENT
6th GRADER

BY MARCUS EMERSON
AND NOAH CHILD

ILLUSTRATED BY DAVID LEE

EMERSON PUBLISHING HOUSE

This one's for Krissy...

My head was spinning, and I had no idea where I was. All I knew for sure was that I was sitting on a chair in a dark room. It was cold, and I could hear water dripping from somewhere behind me. Plus my socks were wet.

Wonderful... I *hate* wet socks.

"Hello?" I tried saying out loud, but my mouth was as dry as uncooked pasta so it only came out as, "*Bleh-bloh?*"

From the shadows across the room, I heard a wooden chair plunk on the floor. "Welcome back, Mr. Brody Valentine," said a boy's voice. "Funny last name you have, isn't it?"

I took a breath and blinked. "There are some things in life we can't choose. Last names… would be one of those things."

"You're right," he replied, stepping forward, but staying hidden in the shadows. "Some of us are just born unlucky, aren't we?"

I remained silent, studying the room while the kid kept talking. From the look of it, I figured I was in a larger storage closet, probably near the school's cafeteria. The smell of steamed broccoli lingered in the air. You'd think that would be proof enough that I was around the lunchroom, but the boy's locker room *also* smelled like steamed broccoli. I *know*, right? *So* nasty.

The boy continued. "When you woke up this morning, you had no idea of the little adventure that awaited you at school, did you?"

I cracked a smile and chuckled softly.

"Unless," the boy whispered, "you *did* know of this adventure, which would mean you're just as guilty as the *rest* of them. Tell me, Brody, *where's* the journal?"

"Someplace safe," I replied as I sat up in my chair. My head was swelling with pain. "Someplace far away from here."

The boy paused. "You know this is over, right? This little game you and your friends are playing… they've already ratted you out. You're *done*."

I wasn't sure if the boy was bluffing or not so I didn't respond. I don't think anyone would've tattled on me, but after the day I've had, I couldn't really be sure. I knew that sixth grade was going to be tough, but not *this* tough. Secret agent stuff, spy gear, special codes, and conspiracies – that was a lot for *anyone* to carry on their shoulders, especially someone like me!

I'm literally a nobody at Buchanan School, or at least, I *used* to be before today. Now it's almost like I'm the most wanted kid in the entire school, and trust me when I say it *wasn't* on purpose.

My name is Brody Valentine and this is the story of how I accidentally became a secret agent. Don't make fun of my last name either. Like I said earlier… there are some things in life we *can't* choose.

I remember it like it was just this morning... probably because it *was* just this morning...

ME
(BRODY VALENTINE)

Check it out – that's my school picture. Scrawny little dweeb, right? Hardly secret agent material. I bet spy agencies have this photo hanging in their offices to show them what kind of person *not* to hire. My parents tell me I have a big heart and that's all that matters, but telling that to a sixth grade boy is the same thing as beating a video game on easy – it's something that takes almost no effort, but at least you can move on to the next game.

I know. I get it. I'm not destined to be a great football player or ultimate fighter, but I accept that. Instead, I'll be the super billionaire computer nerd that controls half of the world and—wait, that makes me

4

sound like an evil villain, but I'm not *that* either.

I'm just an ordinary dude, at a *not* ordinary school called Buchanan. It's important to note that my school is trying this new thing where the sixth graders have the freedom to choose their own classes like they would in middle school. It's a neat idea, but it doesn't make middle school *less* of an adjustment. It just makes sixth grade that much *more* of an adjustment.

I got to Buchanan a few minutes before homeroom. The bus driver always cuts it way too close. Apparently the last stop on his route is a gas station where he gets coffee and donuts for himself. The rest of the students wait in the bus as he sips hot coffee and flirts with the cashier for several minutes. She's *cute*, but seriously? How he still has a job is a mystery to me.

I'm the kid that rushes through the hallways, trying my best not to bump into anyone. You'd only see me if I bonked into you. I usually mumble an apology and keep on going, hoping you don't say anything. Kids would shrug me off as antisocial, but the truth is that I'm just *really* shy.

I was at my locker, placing some books into my backpack. The bell was going to ring in just a few minutes so everyone was rushing through the hallways, doing what they could to be on time.

As I lifted one of my textbooks, I felt a dull ache in my side. Groaning, I dropped the book and stretched my arms back. There was a bruise around my ribcage from gym class the day before. There's a game a few of us play called "Chicken." We're a little too old for the playground at recess, but that doesn't stop us from going over to the monkey bars during gym for this game.

Have you ever played it?

Two people hang from the bars and only use their legs to knock the other person off. Kicking is against the rules, but wrapping your legs around the other person's body isn't. When one kid has a good grip on the other, they try to pull them off the bars. It's not usually dangerous because everyone lands on their feet, but the last time I played I just happened to slip and fall into one of the giant garbage barrels next to the monkey bars, which is how I got the bruise. It was entirely my fault so there weren't any hard feelings.

Over the sound of frantic students, I could hear the morning announcements playing over the speaker system. Large flat screen televisions hung at the end of each hallway and would play an animation of the announcements. Every now and then, it would play a video about keeping the school clean.

A couple weeks ago, someone pulled a prank and hijacked the system, playing a video of a tap dancing cat over and over again. I suspect the televisions are hooked up to a video player somewhere in the building. How else would it be so easy for a dancing cat to get on TV?

As I shut my locker, I heard some students talking nearby.

"Hey," said a boy. "You got any more of that candy?"

"A little bit," a girl replied. "But go get your own! I spent *all* my lunch money on this!"

"But I can't go down there! I still owe them money for the last few candy bars they gave me!" the boy replied.

She chuckled at him. "Then I guess you're outta luck. Looks like you'll have to buy some carrots from the *vending* machines."

The boy sighed. *"Sick..."*

I stood at my locker, staring at the two kids having the conversation.

When the girl noticed me, she looked embarrassed, but it quickly turned to anger. "What are *you* lookin' at?"

I wanted to say something sarcastic like, "A new

alien life form!" but instead, I went with something safer by *actually* saying, "Nothing, sorry."

As I walked away, I hoped that she wouldn't say anything else to me. Thankfully, she didn't.

The class I had homeroom in was past the lobby of the school, where Buchanan had just installed the new vending machines that girl had mentioned. When everyone first heard about them, they were excited and hopeful for bags of hard candy or chocolate bars. You can imagine our disappointment when we found out it was going to be stocked with healthy alternatives to junk food.

They were refrigerated machines filled with bite-sized vegetables, and gluten free snacks. The sweetest thing in them were yogurt covered pecans, which I have to admit can be pretty tasty, but that's after an entire *day* of no sweets.

The girl and boy were talking about *actual* candy though. Sure, the school provided healthy alternatives and was cracking down on junk food in general, but that didn't mean it wasn't available still. You just had to know where to look. I don't know how everyone else can eat so much of it though… too much for me and my teeth start to feel gritty.

As I stepped into the front lobby, I grabbed the straps of my backpack and held tight. Keeping my eyes on the ground, I started walking forward, making myself as limp as possible just in case someone bumped shoulders with me. It was like a jungle out there – boys showcased how tough they were by having the strongest shoulder bumps – it was the sixth grade version of a pecking order.

Y'know what I'm talking about? When there's a group of birds, those birds will single out the weakest member of the bunch and then pick on that poor animal until it's basically kicked out of their circle. The bird that was kicked out doesn't often survive. That's what's called a pecking order. I know, right? Birds can be *jerks*.

I looked up and saw the faces of kids as I walked by, imagining that they had giant beaks for noses. Someone sneezed from a few feet away. I LOL'd because it sounded like a squawk from a chicken.

And then only a half second later, the universe delivered a swift body slam of life changing events right to my door.

"Gangway!" shouted a voice.

I turned around, putting my hands up in case someone was about to run into me. Turns out, my instinct was correct, and a student tackled me to the ground. My backpack gave just enough cushioning that I didn't shatter to bits. "What gives?" I shouted, rolling to my side.

My attacker glanced at me as he stood from the ground, and I recognized him immediately. It was a good friend of mine, Linus. We weren't best friends, and never did anything together outside of school, but he was one of the few geeks I could have a normal conversation with at lunch. And by "normal conversation," I mean we talk about what happens to a zombie if a vampire bites them. He thinks the zombie would be cured because they'd become a vampire. But a zombie's already dead, right? So that means the vampire just sucked zombie blood, which would turn the vampire *into* a zombie!

…anyway, Linus was standing over me.

LINUS

"Sorry, man!" Linus said as he looked down the hallway.

Through some of the students, I saw two hall monitors trying to make their way toward us. Both of them were dressed in black suits and had dark sunglasses over their eyes. None of the monitors I knew ever wore fancy clothing like that, but maybe their dress code had changed.

Linus spun around and scampered down the hall. The *least* he could've done was help me to my feet! I guess he wasn't as good of a friend as I thought.

The two hall monitors flew by me, barely noticing I was there. I sat for a moment, feeling stupid that I was on the floor in the middle of the lobby while other students swarmed around me, rushing to their classes. Not *one* kid stopped to see if I was alright. It was like I was invisible!

Finally, I sighed, setting myself up one of my knees. Luckily none of my fragile bones had been broken during the scuffle. I stood, ready to continue my trek to homeroom, but something fell from my shirt. It surprised me because it sounded like a crinkle from a package.

Staring at the floor, I studied the tiny plastic packet. "What are *you*?" I whispered, half expecting it to speak me. Shaking my head, I rolled my eyes. "I really *do* watch too much television."

The package that fell was a fortune cookie, still contained within its little plastic wrapping. I had no idea where it came from. My family hadn't eaten Chinese food for dinner in, like, a month so it couldn't have been from my home. Did Linus drop it when he smashed into me?

If I had known that cookie was going to change the course of my entire life, I never would've grabbed it from the floor.

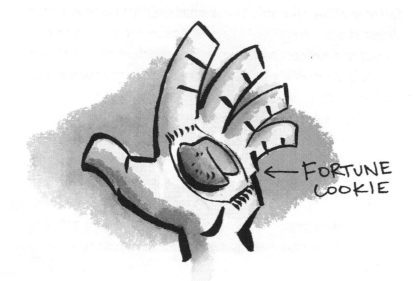

FORTUNE COOKIE

I picked it up, realizing I was the only student in the lobby. Uh-oh, I thought. That was bad news because that could only mean…

The tardy bell suddenly shrieked like a banshee.

"Crumb!" I shouted, clutching at my backpack with one hand and the fortune cookie with my other, completely crushing it by accident.

The bits of cookie were trapped within the plastic packaging. Bouncing it in front of my face, I tried to read the fortune on the little slip of paper inside, but it was weird. It wasn't like any fortune I'd ever seen before. It was a sheet of notebook paper with a handwritten message.

Tearing it open, I let the crumbled pieces of cookie

fall to the floor. I don't like the taste of them anyway so I didn't mind. The slip of paper on the inside was from the corner of a notebook, and even had the light blue lines on it. The back was blank, but the front had numbers written in pencil.

"Do not lose," said the first line.

And the second line read, *"4247.019.5."*

Weird, I thought. It was more of an instruction than a prediction. Normally these things say something about having a bright and shiny day or winning a ton of money, but this one just said *not* to lose. It was more of a warning if anything. You better not lose or else! Or else... *something!*

And what was up with the lucky numbers on the second row? Actually, lucky *number*. The two points in the number meant that it all went together, but what kind of number had two points in it?

"Stop right there!" said a voice from behind me.

My heart skipped a beat. Why didn't I just walk to class? Now I'll probably get busted for skipping! I slipped the sheet of paper into my pocket, and turned around slowly. To my surprise, it wasn't a teacher, but the hall monitors that had just been chasing after Linus.

"Hey, guys," my voice cracked, intimidated.

One of the monitors stepped forward, tugging at the bottom of his suit coat. Then he adjusted his tie and turned his head until his neck cracked. "What do you know of the boy we were chasing after?" he asked coldly.

I shrugged my shoulders. "Nothing really. We sit at

lunch and talk sometimes, but that's about it."

The monitor glanced back at his partner, who curled his lip and shook his head.

"What's this about?" I asked, feeling anxious. "I'm late to class so I should be on my way." I moved forward, but the monitors stepped in front of me, blocking my escape.

"We've seen the two of you and your nerdy conversations during lunch, and sometimes in gym class," said the monitor in a cold whisper. "You'll have to come with us."

I felt confused. "What are you talking about? You watch us talk to each other? That's not the creepiest thing ever," I said sarcastically. "Besides, what's wrong with a little zombie discussion?"

The monitor's face remained expressionless, as if he were a robot. "We can do this the easy way, or the hard way. I'm sure the principal would rather have it be the easy way."

Suddenly I felt sick to my stomach. I guess it *wasn't* about zombies after all. Mentioning that the principal was involved was all I needed to hear. "Fine," I sighed, and then softly said, "To the principal's office we go."

About five minutes later, I was seated on a bench outside an empty art room. The only instruction the monitors gave was to sit on the bench until further notice. Why they hadn't taken me straight to the principal's office was beyond me. Did Principal Davis want to speak to me in the art room? And what in the world was this about anyways?

Leaning against the brick wall, I shut my eyes and tried to calm myself. My heart was racing in my chest like I had just run a seven-minute mile, which if you knew me, you'd know I can't run the mile in under twelve minutes.

Footsteps echoed on the walls of the hallway, and I straightened my posture. I didn't know what kind of trouble I was in that Principal Davis had to get involved, but it couldn't have been good. I kept my gaze lowered, the way a dog does when they know they're in trouble.

"Brody Valentine," said a boy's voice.

I looked up, surprised to see that it *wasn't* Principal Davis, but another sixth grade student that I recognized from a few classes. He was wearing the same suit as the other monitors, but he wasn't wearing glasses. Under one of his arms was a manila envelope. He held his other hand out to me, not to help me up, but to greet me with a handshake.

I grabbed it, and pulled myself off the bench.

The boy faked a smile. "My name is Colton."

When I was to my feet, I suddenly noticed a strong smell that reminded me of my grandpa. I sniffed at the air until I realized it was *Colton* that smelled. It was the way my grandpa smelled when I sat next to him at church. Not stinky, but like he was some sort of vanilla pine tree. "Dude, are you wearing *perfume?*" I asked.

COLTON

Colton furrowed his brow. "It's not perfume, it's *cologne*."

"What's the difference?" I asked.

"Cologne is what *dudes* wear," Colton replied.

"That's just what they call it so guys don't feel embarrassed buying it," I said.

"Nuh uh," Colton said defensively.

I turned my head at him. "Do you spray it on your neck and clothing?"

His eyes narrowed, but he didn't answer.

"Exactly," I sighed. "You're wearing *perfume*."

Colton shook his head and changed the subject. "Looks like you were involved in a little accident this morning, were you not?"

"What *is* this?" I immediately asked. At this point, all I wanted to do was get to homeroom. "Are you a hall monitor? Why are you guys in suits?"

Pointing his open palm to the door of the empty art room, he gestured for me to enter. "All your questions will be answered shortly. If you please, I'd like to ask you a few things about your friend, Linus."

As I walked into the room, I spoke. "Linus? What's the deal with him? Why were your goons chasing after him?"

Colton pulled one of the stools out from under a desk. He dropped the manila envelope on the surface of the table as he took a seat. After taking a deep breath, he said, "It's nothing serious, really."

"Seems pretty serious to me," I said as I sat in the chair across from him. I glanced at the entrance of the room to where the other monitors were stationed and guarding the door. It was obvious that whatever this situation was about *was* pretty serious. In my best "tough guy" voice, I spoke. "Your guys were chasing after him, and now *I'm* being questioned. Tell me who *you guys* are!"

Colton nodded as he patted at the air in front of him. "It's alright, really. I'm part of Buchanan's secret service division of hall monitors, and those 'goons' as you called them are two of my best men."

"So you *are* hall monitors," I said.

"Not really," Colton replied. "We work separate from those other guys."

"Do they even know you exist?"

"Their captain, Gavin, knows," Colton said. "But he's the only one that does."

I slouched in my seat, sighing. "And now *I* know…"

Colton chuckled, and then returned to the subject at hand. "What do you know about Linus?"

"He's a friend," I answered. "We like the same things, but he's one of those guys who I can only talk to about those same things, y'know? Most of the time there's just awkward silence until one of us breaks it with some talk of zombies or space stuff."

Colton flipped open the manila envelope and scribbled notes as I spoke.

"Like, that's literally all we talk about because we have *nothing* else in common," I said, realizing how sad it actually sounded.

Glancing up from his notes, Colton asked, "Has he ever mentioned anything that might've sounded strange to you? Odd?"

This time, *I* chuckled. "He says that vampires *might* actually be a real thing because back in the 1600's, they used to—"

Colton raised his hand to stop me. "That's not what I meant."

I put my hands in my pockets and leaned back

against the desk. "Whatever, man. Don't you think it's *odd* to think that if vampires *were* real, then they'd probably just be—"

"Holy buckets!" Colton said with a burst, obviously flustered. "Anything odd about this *school!*"

"Oh," I sighed. "Be more clear with your question next time. If you're referring to something specific then maybe it's best if you don't phrase your question in such a generic way."

Colton started rubbing his temples. He looked like he was growing impatient. "We *don't* think it was an accident that he tackled you. Did he say something or give you anything?"

I set my hand on my thigh, feeling for the small piece of paper in my pocket. "No. He said sorry, and then took off."

"Did he *give* you anything?" Colton asked, sitting forward.

I shook my head.

"Listen," Colton sighed. "To be honest, I don't know exactly what any of this is about either, okay? All I know is I've been ordered to bring Linus in because he has some sort of journal he carries around with him, but that's it – I don't even know what's *in* the journal. Usually when an order is secret to the point where even *I'm* not allowed to know the details, it means something big is happening."

A journal? All this for a journal?

I stared at Colton's eyes. "So you're just doing your

job?"

"Right," Colton said with a grin. "And you know what? *I don't care* to know the details. They're irrelevant to me… *meaningless*. Linus has something in his possession that's put him on someone's radar and now he's a wanted criminal."

"Wanted criminal?" I asked, confused. What was this, the wild west? Linus said some pretty outrageous things in the few conversations we've had, but never anything that might lead me to think he was a *criminal*. "Who can even issue something like that at this school? The principal?"

Colton shook his head. "My orders come from the president."

The more I heard, the more confused I became. "Sebastian? *President* Sebastian?"

PRESIDENT
SEBASTIAN

President Sebastian was the newly elected school president of Buchanan. He's an easygoing kid with a smile that'll make you trust him with your life. He's also a bit of a smooth talker, which is probably why he won the election so easily. They say he can sell ice to Eskimos. None of the other candidates even had a chance. He's awesome at sports, has a cheerleader girlfriend, is getting an A plus *plus* in social studies, has *never* needed braces, has a thick head of hair, owns two dogs, and somehow has *tons* of money. He's the *perfect* sixth grader.

"What's Linus wanted *for?*" I asked.

Colton sat up and lifted his arms as if he were surrendering. "Don't know, don't care. I just need to find him so if you have any information about where he *is* or where he was *going*, or *anything* else, it would be *appreciated*."

"What's the principal say about all this?" I asked.

"My orders *don't* come from the principal," Colton repeated.

Everything in my body was screaming at me to hand over the fortune from the cookie, but I couldn't bring myself to do it. My leg burned in the spot where the piece of paper was in my pocket. Not literally of course, but you know how your arm will start to itch if you *imagine* there's an itch there? That's what was happening to me.

I'm not sure why I lied to Colton, but I did. Maybe it was because I was bored with being a nobody in the school. Maybe it was because I wanted some kind of action and adventure. Or maybe it's just because I'm dumb. "No. I don't know anything about Linus that might help you."

Colton folded his hands and exhaled slowly. "That's a shame, because you seemed like a kid with common sense." He stood from the desk and cracked his knuckles.

I didn't know what he was planning on doing, and luckily I didn't have to find out. The speaker by the door crackled, and a girl's voice spoke loud and clear. "Colton, to the front office please. Your bike is parked in a tow away zone. Colton, to the front office *immediately*."

"Blazes!" Colton shouted as he hopped off his seat. "My *bike* is in trouble?"

As Colton started walking to the front door of the art room, I managed to sneak a peek at the page he had written notes on. The manila folder was open on the desk next to me. The paper on top was filled with chicken scratched words and doodles that looked like blueprints. Paper clipped to that sheet was my school picture.

What the heck was my picture doing in his folder?

Stopping at the door, Colton flipped around and headed back to the desk. Slapping the folder shut, he slid it along until it fell into his hand. "Don't want to leave this thing sitting out, do we?"

I didn't answer, watching as he left the room. Before he disappeared out of view, I saw him say something to the two monitors guarding the door. They both nodded at him, and he was gone.

I clutched at my backpack and headed to the exit of the art room. One of the monitors turned around and pointed back at the desk.

"Sit tight, Brody," he said. "Colton will be back shortly to finish your questioning."

"This is insane," I said. "I'm missing class right now. Just let me get out of here! If he needs to ask more questions, he can get a hold of me later!"

Suddenly there was a loud *pop* that came from the hallway. It sounded like the slap you hear when someone belly flops into a swimming pool.

The two monitors spun around immediately. I heard the sound of footsteps running on the linoleum flooring of the hallway, and then saw the monitors sprint away from the door.

"Freeze!" I heard both of the monitors shout as they raced away from the art room.

A normal kid would've taken the opportunity to run out the door and get to class, but not *this* kid. I sat in place, frozen in fear at what might happen if I disobeyed the order to sit tight. A few different scenarios went through my head. Detention? Expulsion? Dare I say it… *community service?*

And then a soft voice came from the door. "Brody Valentine!"

I sighed. I was the only kid in the room at that moment – was it really necessary to use my *entire* name?

I looked up and saw a girl poking her head around the doorframe. She was another sixth grader that I was familiar with. Her name was Madison, and every single boy in the school had a crush on her at one time or another. She was athletic, funny, and more popular than anyone I'd ever seen in my life. She was the complete *opposite* of me. So what was she doing saying my name? How did she even *know* my name? Didn't she have better things to do? Like *brush her hair* or something?

"Valentine!" she said as she waved at me. She glanced down the hallway, and spoke in a hushed whisper. "Hurry up!"

I didn't know what to do so I just stared at her. "Huh?"

She sighed, remaining crouched as she snuck over

to me. She grabbed my arm and pulled me to my feet. "Those monitors are gonna be back any second, so we have to hurry!"

I shook my head, trying my best to understand what was happening. "What're you talking about? What's going on? How do you know my name?"

Madison stopped. "We've been watching you for awhile. Linus said you were someone to keep an eye on so... we kept our eyes on you."

A chill ran down my spine. "Is watching me from a distance some kind of *hobby* now? Like 'bird watching,' except it's called '*nerd* watching?'"

Madison didn't answer my sarcastic quip. She held tight to my arm and forced me to follow her to the door. Before stepping out, she looked around the corner to make sure the monitors were out of sight.

"Madison, was that loud popping sound you?" I asked.

She nodded her head. "So was the call from the principal's office. Colton's gonna kick himself when he remembers he doesn't even *own* a bike. And call me *Maddie*. I *hate* Madison."

When the coast was clear, she jumped into the hall and started sprinting in the opposite direction of the two monitors. I did my best to keep up, but this girl was on the track team! She ran like a cheetah!

"Wait up!" I said, clutching at the cramp in my stomach. I staggered behind her, embarrassed. This was worse than gym class!

When we reached the corner where the hallway turned, we stepped into another one of the empty rooms. She shut the door behind us, but didn't flip on the lights.

Maddie didn't waste any time. *"Where's Linus? What have they done with him?"*

My brain freaked out, and all I said was, *"Whaaaa?"*

"Linus!" she said in a harsh whisper. "We know he made contact with you just before he went off the grid – what did he say to you?"

I shook my head, more confused than I'd ever been. "He… he said…," I mumbled. "He said he was sorry for bumping into me! That's it, I swear!"

She clenched her fist and banged it against a desk. "Did you see where he went afterward? Did those monitors catch him?"

"I don't know," I said, honestly. "After he knocked me down, he got right back up and started running again. The monitors ran past me, chasing after him... they didn't even help me up."

"This doesn't make any sense," Maddie repeated under her breath as she paced back and forth. "What about the journal? Did he give you the journal?"

There it was again – the mention of a journal.

"What's the big deal about this kid's journal?" I asked. "Like, his diary or something? What boy keeps a *diary* on him?"

Maddie sneered at me. "It's not a *diary* – it's a *journal!* A place for Linus to keep his notes and illustrations so he can reflect on them later. It's filled with clues and secrets that could bring down the entire *school!*"

At this point, I felt like all this over exaggeration had started boiling over. This was some kind of cruel joke someone was playing on me because I was an easy target. I mean, really? A journal filled with secrets that would tank the school? Yeah, right.

I rolled my eyes. "Okay, I get it. Ha ha, very funny. Let's all make fun of the dweeb who talks about vampires and zombies, huh? What's the deal? Was this some kind of dare from your cheerleader girlfriends?"

Maddie grabbed my shoulder and forced me back. "This is *not* a joke!"

Shocked, I sat perfectly still. Maddie was a lot stronger than she looked, trust me.

"The agency doesn't know for sure because we lost contact with Linus," Maddie continued, "but a lot of us think he's in possession of a disc containing all the passwords to Buchanan's computer system."

"The passwords to the computer systems?" I asked. "Why's that a big deal? What can someone do with those?"

Maddie's eyes flashed with anger. "If those passwords got into the wrong hands, it could mean devastation for every kid here. You could give everyone straight A's, switch school schedules around, change the answers to every test, create fake holidays to get days off... you could even delete permanent records."

I paused. "You mean you can delete kids from existence?"

Maddie nodded. "Existence from the school, yes. It would be like they never attended here. Did Linus give you *anything?*" she asked again.

This time, I decided not to hide the fortune, probably because I was one of those boys who used to have a crush on Maddie. *Used* to? Who am I kidding? I reached into my pocket and pulled out the slip of paper with the fortune on it. "He dropped this," I said, setting the paper on the desk.

Maddie stared at it. "What's that?"

I shrugged my shoulders. "I dunno. I was hoping you could tell me."

She pulled a chair up to the desk and examined the fortune. "He just gave this to you and ran off?"

"Not exactly," I replied. "He dropped a fortune cookie that was still in a plastic wrap. And *then* he ran off. When I opened the package, I found this hand written fortune inside."

"Clever," she said with a chuckle. "It's just like Linus to do something weird like that."

Maddie and Linus must've been close enough to understand when they were being quirky. "I didn't open it on purpose," I said in my defense. "I accidentally crushed it open, and since it was already broken apart..."

"No," Maddie said, "He meant for you to open it. Who can't resist the urge to bust open a fortune cookie when they find one? I hate fortune cookies, but I still crack them apart to get at the paper inside."

"Hey, me too!" I said, excited. "I hate fortune cookies too! Looks like we have something in common, right?"

She stared at me for a moment, and cocked an eyebrow.

I looked away.

"Do not lose," she said, reading the fortune.

"Weird, right?" I asked. "It's like telling us to win at everything."

"It's probably telling us not to *lose* this *paper*," she said softly, chewing her lip.

29

I tightened a smile and did my best not to look as stupid as I felt. "Maybe that too," I said. "That would make more sense, I guess."

"But what about these numbers?" she asked, pointing at the bottom row. "*4247.019.5.* What a strange number to write out. What could that mean?"

"Phone number, maybe?" I suggested.

"Not enough digits," she replied. "There are four numbers before the first point. Then three before the second point, and then one at the end."

"Could he be splitting the numbers up?" I asked. "Could that be his way of listing out *three* numbers?"

"Maybe," Maddie said. "So then the first number would be four two four seven. And then second would be zero one nine, with the last number being five."

I whispered my thoughts out loud. "Four thousand two hundred and forty seven... nineteen—"

"But it's *not* nineteen," Maddie said, interrupting me. "It's *zero* nineteen. Linus intentionally put the zero in there, but *why?*"

I groaned, sliding back into my chair. "*Grrrrrrr, math!* Math is my *worst* enemy!"

Maddie laughed, but continued talking. "So zero one nine, or zero nineteen. What's that mean?"

Raising my eyebrows, I joked. "Maybe it's a combination to some secret safe Linus stashed away."

Maddie's eyes opened wider as she gasped. "That's it! This is a combination!"

I paused. "Huh?"

"You were right," she explained. "It's not zero one nine, but *nineteen*. And I bet it's nineteen *point* five!"

"But you just said Linus probably meant to have the zero in there."

"Right," Maddie said, and then spoke rapidly. "It's zero nineteen point five because it's referring to the *locker* the combination goes to."

"Zero nineteen point five?" I repeated. "You know how crazy that sounds? Buchanan doesn't have lockers that end in *'point five.'"*

"The lower level does," Maddie said. "All the lockers down there are half the size as the ones on the first and second levels. They're stacked on top of each other so the 'point five' refers to the bottom row of lockers. The zero at the beginning of the number refers to which level of the school it's on. Lockers on the first floor start with the number one, and lockers on the second floor start with the number two."

I nodded, finally understanding. "So the zero means it's in the basement."

"Exactly," she said.

"So the combination is the first number?" I asked, still a little confused. "Four two four seven?"

Maddie studied the sheet again. "If we split the numbers into three, we have the answer."

"No more math!" I moaned.

She ignored me. "The first two numbers make forty two – too high for our combinations so the first number *has* to be four. The last two numbers are the same – it would be number forty seven, which is also too high."

"So the combination is four, twenty four, seven?" I asked, feeling proud that I had solved the puzzle. I mean, figured it out *after* Maddie laid it all out for me.

She looked at me suspiciously, and asked, "How *much* did you tell Colton?"

I shook my head. "Nothing! I didn't tell him anything!"

"Did you show him this cookie?"

"No!"

Maddie chewed her lip again, and then spoke. "Did he say anything to you about this?"

I sat silently for a moment, trying to remember something Colton might've said. "No. He didn't say much. Only that Linus had a journal they were looking for, but nothing about what was *inside* it. And he said his orders didn't come from the principal."

Maddie shook her head, sighing. "I'm not surprised about the principal part. Hall monitors are usually controlled by the school's security team. So I guess it looks like *we* are headed to the '*dungeon*,'" she said with a smirk.

Great, I thought, the "*dungeon*," which was the name students used when talking about the lower levels of Buchanan. The only classes down there were band, woodworking, and show choir. And it was the only place in this entire building that I never wanted to see. I considered writing a note to my parents in case I disappeared forever.

"What do you mean, 'we,'" I said sharply. "I'm *not* going down there, and I don't think you should either unless you *want* your photo to be on the back of a milk carton!"

Maddie put one hand on my shoulder, and stared into my eyes. I thought for a moment that she was going to agree with me until she pushed me back against the chair. It hurt.

"Listen up, you little pimple," she whispered. "Unless you're happy sitting quietly in the back row for the rest of your life, you're gonna come with me!"

I clenched my jaw, doing my best to ignore the pain in my shoulder. "I *am* happy as just another face in the crowd!"

Maddie's eyes slowly drew open. "I don't understand. Don't you want to be *more* than just a sixth grade student? Haven't you ever felt like there's *more* to your life?"

"Not really," I whispered.

Shaking her head, Maddie headed for the door. "That's too bad. Linus must've been *wrong* about you."

I stared down, listening to her footsteps on the floor. I know I just told her I didn't feel like there was more to my life, but I was lying. What kid *doesn't* want *more* out of life?

I sit in class and zone out thinking of what I'd do if I even discovered I had superpowers! I stare out the window of my parent's car imagining I'm driving a hover bike in the ditches! I even have a plan set up in case zombies ever invaded my town!

Of course I wanted more from life!

"Wait!" I shouted, much louder than I meant to.

Maddie stopped in the doorway and turned her head. Her smile told me I didn't need to explain myself. "I *knew* you'd change your mind."

Several minutes later we approached the staircase that led into the lower levels. We made it through the hallways of the school because homeroom had just dismissed so the corridors were filled with students going to their first period classes.

The bell rang again just as Maddie and I arrived at the staircase. As I stared into the lower level, it was already obvious that this part of the school hadn't been taken care of like the upper levels. The fluorescent lights along the tiled ceiling were flickering on and off, as if telling us to stay away in Morse code – not that I understood Morse code though.

I grabbed the railing along the wall and started walking down the steps. "So this journal that everyone is after... you say it contains all the passwords to Buchanan's computer system?"

Maddie shrugged her shoulders. "That's what the word on the playground is."

"But that doesn't make any sense," I muttered.

Rolling her eyes, Maddie spoke sarcastically. "Oh right, I guess you're the expert in all of this now, aren't you?"

LOWER LEVEL

My hand gripped the railing tighter. "I'd like to think all my years of playing video games have trained me for this."

She stopped, staring daggers at me. "You think this is a *game?*"

I paused again, crinkling my nose. "...yeah."

"It's *not*," Maddie said, raising her voice. "And you have no idea of what you're up against!"

"You're right!" I said, upset. "I *don't*, and nobody seems to want to give me any answers either! I've been sent on some mission to the dungeon of the school, to where kids have been known to *disappear* from time to time, just to find a locker that *might* or might *not* contain something that could flip Buchanan upside-down!"

Maddie folded her arms and looked off to her side. "Fine," she snipped. "You're right. You deserve to know a little bit about what's happening." She jumped the last few stairs and landed on the floor of the dungeon. As she continued down the hall, she said, "Ask away."

I walked quickly to catch up with her. "First of all, tell me what this is about."

"You know as much as I do about what's happening at the moment," Maddie said. "Linus has a journal that contains some passwords – passwords that others don't want revealed. He's hidden it away because he probably knew the monitors were going to come looking for it."

"Who does Linus work for?" I asked.

"Classified," Maddie answered bluntly.

"Who do you work for?"

"Same people as Linus, but that's still classified," she replied.

I felt my face grow warm. "Then who do those monitors work for?"

Maddie stopped. "The monitors work for Buchanan School. Duh."

Finally, an *actual* answer. "Who's at the top of their chain?"

"The principal," Maddie said, placing her hands on her hips. She glanced farther down the hallway.

"The principal is behind all this?" I asked, shocked. "But Colton said his orders came from the *president*."

Maddie looked back at me as she continued her

path down the dark hallway. "Sebastian? I don't know why he'd be involved in any of this. The last I heard was that the head of Colton's department was Principal Davis."

I didn't know how to respond. Colton told me one thing, and Maddie was telling me an entirely different thing. "Either way," I said, "Principal or president, both are a little unrealistic, don't you think?"

"And yet…" Maddie continued, "Here you are in the dungeon searching for some clues."

I remained quiet as we marched down the dark corridor. The lights continued to buzz overhead as they cast an annoying blue glow. Scanning ahead wasn't helpful at all because it was like the hallway disappeared in shadows the farther I looked.

Kids were sitting on the floor, clutching at their half eaten chocolate bars, sick from sugar shock. I did my best to avoid eye contact.

Suddenly, a taller boy stepped directly in our path. "Hey guys, whatcha lookin' for today?" he asked as he held his opened backpack toward us, presenting a bag filled with candy.

Just from the one second I had to look in the bag, I saw king sized candy bars, extra large suckers, all kinds of individually wrapped hard candy, and more sugar bombs than I'd seen in my life. It was like Halloween.

"Beat it, loser," Maddie said coldly as she stepped around the young boy.

"Come on, man!" pleaded the boy. "If you're down

here, it means you're lookin' for *candy*, and ya ain't gonna find better prices than me!"

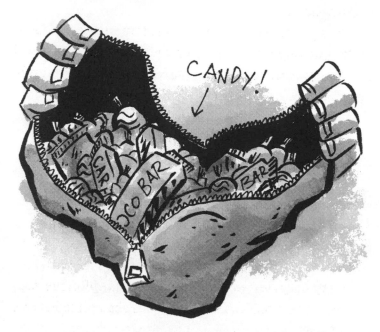

CANDY!

I couldn't look away from the satchel of goodies. I wasn't a sugar addict, but even *I* felt a *little* tempted.

Maddie grabbed my arm and pulled me along. "Brody, we have to go. Don't waste your time with this kid. He isn't worth it."

The boy smiled, exposing the braces over his huge teeth. "You'll be back," he whispered. "It's only a matter of time before you start craving some chocolate covered caramels."

Weird, I thought, because the instant he said it, I actually started craving them. I shook my head, to clear my mind from thoughts of candy. Then I spoke to Maddie again. "I had no idea the candy problem was this bad down here."

"It's gotten worse over the last few weeks," Maddie replied, studying the numbers on the lockers as we passed them. "Funny 'cause this wasn't much of a situation until they installed those vending machines upstairs."

"Sebastian really pushed for those machines too," I added. "You'd think he'd try his best to curb what was happening down here."

Maddie raised an eyebrow. "I don't think he saw it coming. None of us really did."

I scanned the crusty tiles on the ceiling as I followed her, but then bumped into her back. She had stopped walking before I noticed. I stumbled a bit, trying to keep my balance, but also because I was embarrassed.

"Pay attention," she whispered as she pointed at one of the lockers on the bottom row. "Look. Nineteen point five."

I stared at the locker. Green paint chipped off and revealed a rusted sheet of metal underneath. The combination padlock had cobwebs hanging from it, probably from never being used. "Gross," I said.

Maddie rolled her eyes at me. "Grow up," she said as she put her fingers through the cobwebs. "It's just some spider webs. It's nothing to be—"

Instantly, she drew her hand back and squealed so loudly that my ears hurt. Jumping up and down and wildly flapping her hands, she yelled, "Something touched my fingers! There's a spider in there! *Sick sick sick sick sick!"*

I laughed, clutching at my stomach. *"Grow up,"* I said, mocking her voice.

She slapped my shoulder and giggled, catching her breath. Then she nodded toward the locker. "Take care of it," she said with a smile.

I quickly wiped away the webs and smeared my hands across my jeans to make sure none of the demon creatures were crawling on me. I *hate* spiders.

Maddie knelt down and started twisting the lock in circles, entering the combination. After she was done, she glanced at me as she pulled up on the handle.

Click.

The door to the locker pushed out about half an inch. Maddie took a breath, and then flipped it open the rest of the way.

I didn't know what to expect, but I braced myself for anything. And by "braced myself for anything," I mean I covered my face and dove to the ground, whimpering like a puppy.

"Would you get up?" Maddie growled, whispering. "What's the *matter* with you?"

The cold floor was against my body as I looked up. Other kids from down the hall were staring at me like I was a crazy person. Look at what I've been reduced to... laying in the basement of Buchanan School while sugar addicts felt sorry for *me.*

"Get up already!" Maddie ordered. "You're

embarrassing me!"

I pushed myself off the ground, and dusted off the front of my shirt. Cracking my neck like a boss, I approached locker nineteen point five. Peering inside, I saw a very disappointing sight – at the bottom of the dusty locker was a single yellow crayon, but that was it. There was *nothing* else.

"Serious?" I sighed.

Maddie picked up the crayon and inspected it. "Look here at the bottom," she said, pointing the butt of the crayon at my face. "The number sixty two is etched into it."

"Did Linus scratch that in there?" I asked. "Some more secret code stuff?"

Maddie nodded.

"This is all so anti-climactic," I groaned. "I thought

at least there would be some kind of secret spy box filled with junk to play with."

Lowering the crayon, a smile cracked across Maddie's face. Then she set her foot into the locker and pushed down until it clicked. Instantly, the back wall of the locker unbolted and slid out of view. A small black bag rolled from the container and flopped onto the floor.

"There's your secret spy box," she said.

"Whoa," I said, unzipping the bag. The inside wasn't filled with much, but it was still the coolest treasure I'd ever seen. There was a pack of stink bombs, a pad of blank hall passes, an old school wrist watch, a pair of glasses with a fake nose and mustache, and a stack of one-dollar bills.

Maddie continued to keep an eye out. "Strap on the watch," she said. "It's also a walkie talkie."

My heart skipped a beat as I tightened the watch to my wrist. I felt like I was a secret agent suiting up for a deadly mission. "Who else has a watch like this?"

Another smile appeared on Maddie's face as she pulled her sleeve up, exposing the exact same watch that I was now wearing. "They come in handy," she said. "Trust me."

I looked at the yellow crayon in her hand. "So what's the deal with that thing?"

Maddie sighed. "It's a code. Yellow, sixty two."

"Another locker?" I asked.

"No," she said, shaking her head. "They're instructions, but there's only one person in the school that

42

can decipher it."

I remained silent, waiting for Maddie to continue.

"Sibyl," Maddie said.

"Sibyl?" I asked. I never met anyone at Buchanan named Sibyl. "Okay. So who is she and where's she at?"

"She's a fortune teller, and on *our* team," Maddie replied as she started walking deeper into the basement of Buchanan. "And *we* don't find her. She finds *us*."

About ten minutes later and several turned corners in the basement, we were far enough away from the steps for me to know that if I lost Maddie, I'd be lost in the dungeon forever.

The farther we went, the darker it became. Sugar addicts were all over the place, mumbling nonsense as their bodies went through various stages of a sugar crash.

"I feel sorry for these kids," I said, following Maddie through the halls.

Maddie sighed. "It won't last long. As soon as lunch rolls around, these kids will get some proper food in their bellies and be fine again. But you're right. Up until lunchtime, this is a sad sight."

My legs were starting to burn from all the walking. "So where's this Sibyl kid you were talking about? If *she* has to find us, then why all the walking?"

"She has her own base, so to speak," Maddie explained. "But it's not like she's sitting behind a desk or anything. She has to be called upon."

"Like with a phone?" I asked.

"No," Maddie continued. "She can only be called in the girl's restroom down here."

"Um, what?"

"In the girl's restroom, all of the toilets have to be flushed at the same time," Maddie said. "That's the code we follow when we need her help."

"So weird," I whispered.

The lighting in this section of school came completely from the fluorescent bulbs above us. Without any windows, the lower levels were a dark and depressing place. I started to understand why others called it the "dungeon."

Finally, we reached a water fountain with swinging doors on both sides of it. The signs on the doors were hand written with the word *"boys"* on one and *"girls"* on the other. I wasn't surprised to see an *"out of order"* sign hanging from the fountain.

Maddie turned and pointed her finger at me. "Wait out here, and *don't* talk to anyone."

I nodded. "Roger that, ten four."

"Nerd," Maddie whispered, pushing the door to the girl's bathroom open.

When the door shut, I slipped my hands into my pockets and leaned against the cold lockers on the wall. The hallway we were in wasn't any different from the rest of the hallways in the dungeon – they were all equally terrifying. I was beginning to second-guess my decision for adventure and excitement. Maybe being left all alone in the dark had something to do with it.

"Hey, kid," came a thick whisper from the shadows.

I held my breath, staring into the dark, doing my best to see what kind of *monster* I was about to get attacked by. My brain froze, but I knew if I sounded scared, then I would appear weak. "Heeee.... Heeeeeee.... Heeeeeeeeeeeeeeeello?" Yeah, that didn't sound weak at all.

A boy dressed in a suit stepped out of the darkness, and approached me. It was Colton, but his two henchmen weren't with him. Somehow, I was relieved that it wasn't another kid trying to sell me candy, but all the relief washed away when I remembered I had just escaped from him only moments ago.

I stepped forward, afraid to say anything, so I just stared at him like a baby seeing fireworks for the first time.

Colton raised his open palms at me and shook his head. "No, it's alright. I'm not lookin' to bring you in or anything."

His big blue eyes told me he was being honest. "Then what? Did you guys follow me down here?"

"We've been following you for awhile," Colton said. "But that's not the point, and we don't have a lot of time before your girlfriend comes out of that bathroom with Sibyl."

"She's *not* my girlfriend," I said, feeling more disappointed than I'd ever admit. "If you know about all this, and you're not trying to stop it, then what *do* you want?"

Colton shook his finger at me. "By now you know a little more about the situation, so I wanna give you another chance to *help* me."

"Help you?"

"Mm hmm," Colton hummed. "You're gonna find that journal for us, and when you do, you're gonna hand it over along with the rest of the kids you're workin' with."

"Why would I do that?" I asked, folding my arms tightly.

"Because I'll make sure you're seen as the hero. President Sebastian has even said there's money for you if you help us," Colton said, bluntly.

I knew he wasn't lying. There were kids in the school who had rich *parents*, but Sebastian was actually rich *himself*. He had money, and wasn't afraid of flaunting it. Maybe being the school president came with perks... like a paycheck.

Colton continued. "Let's say you find that journal. And then let's say you do whatever it was Maddie and Linus were planning on doing with it. What do you think would happen to *you*? You honestly think you won't be expelled the instant that journal comes to light? Do you even know whose side you're on?"

I didn't want to believe him, but part of me did. I truly had no idea what side I had taken when I came to the dungeon with Maddie. Was it possible that I was working with the bad guys?

Behind the wooden door of the girl's restroom came the sound of all the toilets flushing at once. It was the signal Maddie used to get Sibyl's attention.

Colton's eyes shot at the door as he stepped back into the shadows. He pointed his finger at me one last time and spoke. "When you find that journal, you bring it straight to us. *Don't* listen to anything Maddie says to you, and *don't* open that journal."

I stepped forward, wanting to confess that I *wasn't* the action hero I was pretending to be. "But..."

Colton interrupted me. "*We're* the good guys, Brody. Get us that journal, and we'll make sure you're seen as the hero."

And then the hall monitor slipped away in the shadows of the dungeon. If this were a movie, I would've thought that was awesome, but this wasn't a movie, and I only felt creeped out.

The bathroom door swung open, and Maddie stepped out. A girl walked through the door after her and smiled at me. This must be Sybil, I thought.

SIBYL

She had a very clean complexion under her short blond hair. She couldn't have been any younger than us, so I figured she was in the sixth grade too. At her side hung a beat up leather satchel.

"My name is," I started to say, but Sybil interrupted

me.

"Brody, yes, I know," Sybil said.

"Wow! You *already* knew my name!" I said. "You really *are* a fortune teller!"

Sybil rolled her eyes and glanced at Maddie. "No, Maddie told me you were waiting outside the bathroom for us."

"Oh," I said, lowering my head. "So do you just hang out in the bathroom all day, waiting for someone to flush all the toilets at once?"

Sibyl sighed. "No."

"Huh," I grunted.

"Maddie tells me you're quite the agent," Sibyl said, changing the subject. "On your way to becoming a real hero, aren't you?"

"Not really," I replied. "I'm just sorta tagging along. We'll see how much of a hero I turn out to be when this is all over."

Sibyl smiled softly. "Every journey starts with a single step, right?" she asked. "And a hero is born *during* the journey – *not* at the end of it."

The tiny amount of confidence I felt from Sibyl's words was enough to create a warm feeling in my chest.

Sibyl held her hand out to Maddie. "Let me see the clue Linus left for you."

Maddie reached into her pocket and pulled out the yellow crayon. She held the bottom out toward the fortune teller and spoke. "Sixty two. That's what's scratched into the bottom of this."

Sibyl took the crayon in her hand and stuck out her lower lip, studying the piece of colored wax. She hummed a tune I didn't recognize. It must've been her way of thinking. Finally, she said, "I haven't seen one of these since the second grade. Strange that Linus would use such an old school puzzle."

"Can you decode it?" Maddie asked.

Sibyl smiled. "My name is *Sibyl*, isn't it?"

I felt confused. "What's that mean? What does your name have to do with this?"

The fortune teller turned toward me and spoke. "Everyone's name means something. Sibyl actually means *'fortune teller.'* Cool, huh?"

"Whoa," I whispered, and then turned toward Maddie. "What's *your* name mean?"

Maddie looked up at me, frowning. "Madison means nothing. It's just the city I was born in. My parents weren't too creative."

"How about me?" I asked, excited.

Sibyl shrugged her shoulders. "How am I supposed to know? I don't memorize the meaning of every single name. I have better things to do!"

"Right," Maddie said, irritated. "And right now we need to decode Linus's message."

Sibyl agreed, reaching into her satchel. After fishing around for a second, she removed a gadget that was made from a folded sheet of paper. It looked like a pyramid. "This is an origami fortune teller."

I recognized it immediately after she said it. "I

50

remember playing with those back in the day!"

Maddie scratched at her cheek. "If this is such an old school technique that Linus is using, how do we know that the information inside that will be helpful?"

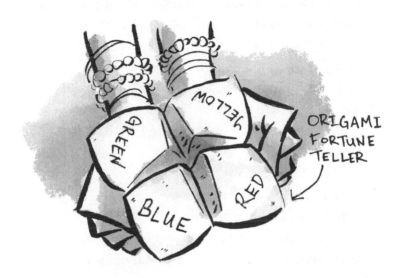

ORIGAMI FORTUNE TELLER

"The information inside this device will last forever," Sibyl explained. "In twenty years, if someone leaves the same clue as Linus did, it'll still point in the right direction."

"If I'm *still* a sixth grader in twenty years," I said, "I'll be pretty bummed out."

The two girls just stared at me. I guess I wasn't as funny as I thought.

The origami fortune teller Sibyl was holding had writing all over it. The four corners on the outside each had a color. The inside had numbers, and other scribbling. Linus's crayon must've had the correct path to take on the device in order to get to the message he wanted to deliver.

Maddie held the yellow crayon up again. "Yellow is the first instruction."

Sibyl put her fingers in the bottom of the fortune teller and started flipping the device apart each time she said a different letter. "Yellow – Y – E – L – L – O – W." When she was finished she looked at Maddie, waiting for the next instruction.

"It's not sixty two," Maddie said.

"No," Sibyl said. "It's the number six and the number two." She flipped the origami fortune teller in and out as she counted. "1 – 2 – 3 – 4 – 5 – 6."

At last, Maddie said, "Two."

Sibyl winked at me as she opened the flap with the number two on it. She looked down and read it quietly while moving her lips.

"What's it say?" Maddie asked excitedly.

"Lower than a chicken's garbage," Sibyl whispered.

Maddie's eyes slowly panned upward. I could almost see the gears grinding in her head as she tried to understand what Sibyl had just said.

"That's it?" I asked. "Is that another riddle or something?"

Sibyl tightened her lips and looked at me. "Every answer in this is a riddle that leads to another location."

"After so many years, wouldn't you already know the answers to each riddle?" Maddie asked.

"This thing has only been used twice," Sibyl replied. "I've never landed on this flap before."

At that moment, the bell started ringing, signaling the end of first period. The hallway we were standing in soon became a flurry of students rushing to make it to their next class. Because there were so many children, a couple spots in the herd moved slower than others. It was like rush hour, but with kids instead of cars.

When I turned to ask Sybil more questions, she was gone.

Maddie placed her hands on her hips. "Lower than a chicken's garbage," she repeated patiently as she watched people walk by. "What could that mean?"

"I have no clue," I replied.

Maddie took the lead and started moving down the hallway. Hopefully she was headed for the stairs so we could leave the dungeon. Weaving in and out of other students, I stayed as close to her as possible, doing my best not to lose her.

Every few feet I saw some kids opening candy bars and taking monster bites out of them. There were even a few teachers munching on some sweet treats as they stood by their classroom doors.

"Where are we going?" I asked Maddie.

She didn't break her stride. "To the gymnasium," she said.

"The gym? Is that what you have for second period?"

"No, but we'll be able to hang out there while we

try to figure this riddle out. Mr. Cooper is pretty cool like that."

I laughed. "Cool like that? Or just doesn't give a spew about taking attendance?"

I couldn't see Maddie's face, but I could tell from her voice that she was smiling. "Both."

A few minutes later, we were out of the dreadful dungeon and on the first level of the school. We sped by the front lobby. Kids had already filtered into their second period classrooms, leaving the hallways almost empty.

"Hurry up!" Maddie ordered. "We're going to be late!"

My side started to cramp again. How in the world do athletes work through pain like this, I thought. "Late to what? A class we're not even supposed to be in?"

"You're an agent today," she snipped. "The principal will understand."

At that moment, my shoulder accidentally bumped shoulders with someone else. I stared at the ground, afraid of who it was that I unintentionally challenged.

"Sorry, man," said a boy. "Didn't see ya there."

Relieved, I looked up. It was another sixth grader that I recognized from my last period class, English. His name was Chase Cooper. "Sorry, Chase. I hope I didn't hurt you."

Chase grinned, rubbing his shoulder. "It's not a problem," he said. "I mean, my *ninja* skills might be affected, but for only a day."

I laughed at his joke. *Ninja* skills? Can you imagine that? Ninjas at Buchanan School? *That'll* be the day.

"Chase, are you coming?" a girl shouted from the other end of the lobby. It was Zoe, his cousin.

Chase leaned over and waved. "Yeah, I'll be right there," he shouted. Then he stepped past me and nodded. "See ya, dude."

"See ya," I replied.

Maddie watched as he walked away. "You know that kid?"

"Yeah," I said. "He's a pretty cool guy."

She watched Chase as he walked away, and then looked at me. "There's more to him than you might think."

"Like what?"

"It's classified," she said, turning away. "Maybe someday you'll be allowed to view his file, but not today."

I raised my eyebrows and shook my head, confused. "Whatever."

Before we could make it any farther in the lobby, the school bell rang out like a bell because well... it *was* a bell.

"Wonderful," Maddie groaned as she stopped in the middle of the lobby. She turned toward me and held her hand out. "Gimme your backpack."

I tightened my fists around my straps. "What? Why?"

"We don't have any time," she said quickly. "Just give it to me!"

I stared at her, unflinchingly. "What do you need? Just tell me and I can—"

Suddenly, a voice erupted from behind us. "Excuse me!"

I froze up instantly.

Let me explain something again real quick – I'm not the most adventurous kid in the world. I like my days predictable and boring. Boring is good – there's no *trouble* in boring. I'm not *un*popular, but I wouldn't say that I'm a loser. I'm just your average, stereotypical dude trying his best not to attract attention, y'know what I mean? I *just* want to get through sixth grade unnoticed and unharmed.

That's why getting caught outside of class caused me to freeze up.

"What're you two doing out here?" the adult's voice asked from behind us. "*Hall passes*, please."

I slowly turned to face my certain death. It was Mrs. Olsen, the science teacher. I wanted to throw the question right back at her and ask her why *she* was outside of class, but I knew that would guarantee a day's worth of detention. I started mumbling a response, "Um, we just… uhh…"

I felt Maddie yank my backpack off of me. She leaned closer and whispered. "Distract her for a second."

My heart raced as I tried to think of something to distract Mrs. Olsen with. I wasn't good at this sort of thing! "I'm glad you're out here!"

Mrs. Olsen's lips pressed together as she folded her arms. "And why is that?"

"Because," I started saying, feverishly trying to think of something clever, "I had a question about last night's assignment."

"Oh really?" Mrs. Olsen asked, suspicious. "Last night's assignment is due today, and you have science... what period?"

"Fourth," I answered, "but I've got study hall before that so I thought I could ask you and finish it up during that."

Mrs. Olsen sighed as she waved her fingers toward herself. "Alright then. What is it?"

If I could remember what the assignment was, it probably would've helped. Instead of saying anything else, I stared at her as air slowly escaped from my throat. "It was abouuuuuuuuut..."

Sweat started to collect on my forehead, and was about to drip down my nose at any second. *Where was Maddie? There's no way I can stall Mrs. Olsen any longer!*

Thankfully, another adult came to my rescue, but I had no idea who it was. It was just a guy who came outta nowhere! He stepped out from behind me and held a slip of paper between his dainty fingers. I had to hold back a chuckle because the guy looked so goofy. He had a thick pair of glasses over a fat nose and a bushy mustache, and then I realized... it was *Maddie* in disguise.

"Hello, madam," Maddie said with a gruff voice. The way she changed her voice was both impressive and terrifying. "This *upstanding* student must have left my classroom *without* his hall pass."

"Wait," Mrs. Olsen said, leaning to one side. "Weren't there two of you out here?"

I shrugged my shoulders, playing along with Maddie's disguise. "Nope, it was just me. No idea what you're talking about."

"Hmmmmm," Mrs. Olsen hummed, stone-faced as she took the paper from Maddie's hand. "And who exactly, are *you?*" she asked the bushy mustached man.

Maddie's eyes darted back and forth. "My name is Misterrrrrr…" she trailed off trying to come up with a name.

"Misterrrrrrr?" Mrs. Olsen repeated as she cocked an eyebrow.

Maddie snapped her head up. "*Five!* The name is Mister *High Five!* I'm a substitute teacher today, thank you very much."

Mrs. Olsen curled her lip. "Oh really? *Mister High Five?*"

I stared at Maddie hoping she knew what she was doing.

"Are you going to make fun of my name as well?" Maddie asked, upset. "I'll have you know I get a lot of that, and you'd think I'd have developed thicker skin because of it, but I *haven't*. Go on then, make fun of me *all* you want, but at least have the decency to do it to my *face*."

Mrs. Olsen's expression went from suspicious to sympathetic as she mumbled. "I'm sorry, I didn't mean to offend you. It's just a rather odd name, and…" Mrs. Olsen paused. "You know what? You're absolutely right. It's a *fine* name, Mister High Five."

Maddie lifted her chin proudly. "Thank you. Now if you'll excuse me, I must be getting back to my class, and I believe young little Brody Valentine should be as well?" she asked, bouncing her eyebrows up and down.

"Yup!" I snickered.

Pressing her lips together again, Mrs. Olsen waved

me away. "Fine. Get to class."

I took the hall pass from her hand and smiled. "Thanks, Mrs. Olsen. See you later."

The teacher nodded, and continued onward to her classroom.

I spun around, in awe of Maddie's quick thinking. "That was *brilliant*," I said.

"Ya think?" she replied. "And also – nice drawings."

My heart sunk. I didn't want her to dig through my backpack because I had a folder filled with doodles of superhero costumes that I only worked on during study hall. I've never showed them to anybody because it was a little embarrassing.

With a smirk, she added, "Don't worry about it. They're cool. It shows me that you really do dream of bigger things."

"A couple of lame drawings told you that?"

"Not exactly," she said, "but the superhero drawing that had an arrow to the words *'my costume'* did."

I slapped my forehead. "*Why* did I write that?"

"I said don't worry about it," Maddie replied. "Everyone daydreams like that. Nobody ever *talks* about it, but we *all* do it. Even me."

Taking a breath, I smiled. Instead of feeling embarrassed by her advice, I actually felt comforted. Madison was one of the more popular kids in the school, and to hear her admit something like that was pretty cool of her.

Another few minutes later, and we were standing in the middle of the gymnasium. Mr. Cooper, the gym teacher, was making his rounds as usual. And like always, he seemed distracted as he scratched the attendance off his clipboard.

He was so absentminded that when he approached Maddie and I, he didn't miss a beat. "Maddie... Brody..." he said, scratching checkmarks off the attendance sheet. I had no idea where he put the checkmarks because I knew our names *weren't* on his sheet of paper. We weren't even supposed to be in that class!

Mr. Cooper blinked slowly as he spoke. "Basketball in here, soccer and walking the track are outside. Do whatever, I don't even care anymore."

"See?" Maddie said, heading toward the gymnasium doors. "That man doesn't pay attention to anything. There's nothing to worry about."

"Where are you going?" I asked, jogging to catch up.

"To walk around the track and think," she answered. "Some fresh air might do us some good."

Just as Maddie stepped outside, I turned to make sure Mr. Cooper hadn't caught on to our scheme. He was already in his office, leaning back in his chair with his feet propped up on a desk. I guess Maddie was right. There was nothing to worry about.

Well, almost nothing. This whole situation was

something to worry about, wasn't it? I'm following a girl around the school searching for a journal that contains secrets that Buchanan's president is willing to *pay* for. Not to mention being followed by Colton and his hall monitor goons.

Maddie walked in front of me as she spoke quietly to herself. Should I tell her about Colton cornering me in the dungeon? Should I fill her in on the details of what he said just before Sibyl had come out of the bathroom? Was Colton even the *bad guy?* Before he disappeared like a vampire, he said he was working for the *good guys.* Could it be that Maddie and Linus were the bad guys in all this? Was I on the wrong team?

"You coming?" Maddie yelled, annoyed. She was almost twenty feet ahead of me.

I must've stopped walking. I sometimes do that when my brain is running a million miles an hour. It's like it can't do two things at once. "Yeah, sorry."

On the track, she walked next to me as she continued to repeat the strange fortune Sibyl had read. "*Lower* than a chicken's garbage…"

"Do chickens even *have* garbage?" I asked.

"Maybe? What's in a chicken coop?"

"Chickens," I answered. "And their eggs and stuff… I *think.*"

"Do chickens eat anything that's packaged? The packages would need to be thrown away, right? So *that* could mean it was the chicken's garbage."

I chuckled at the thought of a chubby chicken

eating some cheese sticks out of a container, and then burping as they patted their belly filled with food. In my head, the chicken carelessly tossed the container over its shoulder.

"What's so funny?" Maddie asked.

"A burping chicken," I answered.

"You wanna grow up and join the real world for a second?" she snapped, lightly punching at my shoulder.

Her punch pushed me enough that my ribs ached. The smile disappeared from my face as I flinched. "Careful," I said. "I've got a killer bruise on my side."

Maddie continued walking on the track. "From what?"

I shook my head, trying to avoid the embarrassing story of my injury. "It's stupid. Some guys were just playing on the monkey bars the other day…"

"The monkey bars? Aren't those on the other side of the school? Where the first graders have recess."

I scratched at the back of my head. "Yeah, but we don't play on them or anything. I mean, we do, but not in the same way."

"You don't swing from them?"

I kept my pace with her as I replied. "No, we do, but not like them. You see there's a game we play called…" and then my brain connected the dots. "*Chicken.*"

Maddie turned toward me. "That's a *dumb* game."

I ignored her biased opinion. "But I hit my side on the garbage can next to the monkey bars!"

Finally, Maddie understood. "Wait. You mean there's a garbage can next to the monkey bars?"

"A rusty metal one. It's like a giant barrel."

"A chicken's garbage," Maddie said, thinking. "It's a stretch, but I can't see what else that might mean."

"*Lower* than a chicken's garbage," I added. "So... *under* the garbage can maybe?"

Maddie punched my shoulder again, harder this time. With a confident smile and twinkling eyes, she said, "That's it. There's only one set of monkey bars over there. Let's go."

Ten minutes later, we were clear on the other side of Buchanan school. Mr. Cooper was still in his office, so he didn't notice that we had snuck away. Since it was only second period, none of the first, second, or third graders were outside, and the yard was completely empty.

The blacktop was warm, soaking the heat from the sun as it glared down from above in a cloudless sky. We followed the yellow paint markings of the outdoor basketball court as hoops lined the way to the other side of the playground.

Also littered on the ground were empty packages of chocolate bars and other sweets along with random dark spots of flattened chewing gum.

Maddie studied the pavement as she ran. "Looks like this whole candy problem has found its way to the *younger* students as well."

As we approached the monkey bars, we slowed down. The huge barrel was still sitting next to the playground equipment, nestled in a pile of woodchips.

Without hesitating, Maddie grabbed the sides of the garbage can and tipped it over on its side. It hit the earth with a thump.

Suddenly, I heard a buzzing sound all around me, and I freaked out. Sprinting away from Maddie and the barrel, I made it about twenty yards before I turned around. In a matter of seconds, I had traveled the entire course of the playground. Maddie had her hands on her hips and was glaring at me. At least I think she was – it was hard to tell because she was so far away.

"What's your problem?" she shouted.

I cupped my hands over my mouth and yelled.

"*Bees!* I'm allergic to *bees!*"

And seriously, I am. If a bee stings me, I can say goodbye to the rest of my day since it'll be spent in the hospital.

Maddie threw her arms out, angry. "You nimrod! It was just a bunch of fruit flies."

I slouched over, catching my breath, thankful that there weren't actually bees chasing after me. I could feel my heart pounding through my chest as I jogged back to Maddie.

Breathing heavily, I said, "It's just that bees scare me. Like, *really* scare me. Like, if you asked me what the scariest thing in the world is, I would say a giant bee chasing after me on a motorcycle, while his bee buddies scream my name from both sides of the road."

"What an *odd* thing for you to say," Maddie whispered.

I lowered my head, shamed.

Maddie sighed. "No, I understand. My little brother is allergic to them too. It's bad if he gets stung. I was only mad 'cause you took off like a shooting star and scared the daylights out of me."

I laughed. "Scare someone as tough as you? Yeah, right."

She slapped my shoulder playfully. "Whatever," she said, and then pointed at the spot that was under the barrel. "So look what we just found."

Half buried in the moist dirt was a soggy, oversized clear baggie, with something big on the inside, about the size of a textbook. It *had* to be the journal!

Maddie picked up the baggie and ripped it apart. A leather journal slipped out and fell into her hands. "This is it!"

My knees started to shake at the excitement of it all. Finally, after spending half the morning solving clues we were going to see what was inside that stupid thing!

Maddie flipped it over, but the look of delight disappeared from her face. "There's a lock on the front of it. Dang it, Linus!"

Disappointed, I took the journal from her hands and inspected the lock. There was a spot for a small key on the front. But then I noticed a slip of paper sticking out from the top of the journal. "What's this?"

Maddie pinched the paper, and pulled it out. It looked like there was handwriting on the front of it. She squinted, reading the next clue out loud. "The eagle's nest of Principal Davis's office at 9:00 PM."

I threw my arms out wide, frustrated. "Come on, Linus! How many breadcrumbs do you have to leave behind before you just give us the stinkin' answer!"

Crumpling the last clue in her hands, I could tell Maddie was fed up with Linus's little game as well. "Seriously, this kid might be taking it too far now. Whatever's inside this journal better be something *good.*"

"Let's just break that lock apart!" I suggested.

Maddie studied the lock again, and then spoke. "This is a pretty heavy duty piece of metal. You couldn't break it open with a hammer. Trying would just hurt the journal itself, and I don't want to risk that."

"The passwords to Buchanan's computers might be worth a lot, but is it really worth all this trouble?" I asked. "It just doesn't make sense to me!"

"I think this journal could be sold for a ton of money if it got into the wrong hands," Maddie said. "Plus it could throw off the entire grading curve if it were released to the public."

"But that's just it," I said. "It's not like the teachers of the school couldn't create new passwords. As soon as everyone realized that *every single password* had been *compromised*, wouldn't you think that Buchanan would simply change them?"

Maddie paused. "You've got a point," she said, chewing her lip again. "All this trouble for a list of passwords *doesn't* make sense, which might mean there's more at stake than we know."

I pointed at Maddie's fist with the crumpled up clue. "Principal Davis's office is next up, right? Maybe we'll find the answer in there."

"I have a knot in my stomach about it," Maddie added. "If Linus went through the trouble of hiding his journal in the principal's office, then it could mean Principal Davis *himself* could be involved somehow."

"Isn't the principal a *good guy?*" I asked, feeling the same knot twist in my stomach.

"I don't know anymore," Maddie replied as she headed back toward the school. "Maybe this goes all the way to the top. That would explain Colton's involvement."

"But he said—" I coughed, realizing I said too much.

Maddie faced me. The look on her face told me she

wasn't going to let me stop talking. "*What* did Colton say? Earlier, you told me he didn't say *anything* to you."

I still didn't know who to trust, so I lied to Maddie. I didn't tell her that Colton had cornered me in the dungeon. "I mean, he just said his orders didn't come from the principal. I told you that earlier."

Maddie's eyes darted back and forth as if she were connecting invisible dots. "If Colton says his orders don't come from Principal Davis, then maybe the principal *is* in on it."

"Does it have to be connected?" I asked. "Could any of this be a coincidence?"

"Could be," Maddie replied softly. "But what if Colton is trying to bring the principal down?"

The knot in my stomach twisted harder. All of this searching had been a boiled down version of a treasure hunt, but now we were involving adults – adults with *power* – into the game. I didn't like that. "We're getting ahead of ourselves," I said. "It's still possible that the journal just contains passwords. If that's all that's in there, it's not that big of a deal."

Maddie turned around and started heading back toward the entrance of the school. "Only one way to find out."

I took a deep breath, and then followed behind her. This wasn't a game I liked playing anymore. Not one bit.

Several minutes later, we were standing outside the hallway to Principal Davis's office. The corridor was completely empty as we scanned the area. The hall monitors were nowhere to be seen, but that only meant it was a matter of time before their rounds brought them back this way.

"So what's the plan?" Maddie whispered.

"The plan?" I asked. "*You're* the one with actual secret agent experience! What do *you* think the plan should be?"

Maddie looked at me. "You're gonna have to go in there."

"*Me?*" I asked loudly. Cupping my hand over my mouth, I waited a moment before speaking again. "There's no way I'm gonna break into the *principal's office!* I'm already in *enough* trouble for the day! If I get caught doing this, then I'm probably looking at actual jail time!"

"Quit being such a drama queen," Maddie laughed.

"Why aren't *you* the one who's gonna break into there?"

"Because I'll be too busy keeping watch out here! You weren't too useful when Mrs. Olsen caught you earlier, and I doubt you'll be useful now! So if you're behind a closed door, you'll probably be just fine."

"Alone in there?" I asked. "Are you nuts?"

Lifting her wristwatch, she spoke. "I'll be with you through this. Remember that they're communicators."

All the fear washed away from my body as I remembered the cool spy watch on my arm. "Oh right! Okay, I'll *do* it!"

Maddie glanced down both ends of the hallway, and then walked to the principal's office door. Turning the handle silently, she pushed it open half an inch. She pressed her faced against the open slit, and let the door shut again. "Davis isn't in there. You're good to go."

I handed her my backpack. "What do I do when I'm in there?"

"You'll tell me everything you see," Maddie said, pulling my bag over her shoulders. "Then I'll be able to walk you through the rest."

"What about the last clue?" I asked.

Maddie pulled a tight smile and shrugged her shoulders. "Without knowing what's in there, I can't help you. Once you're inside, maybe you'll understand the clue better," she said. And then she repeated the riddle. "The eagle's nest of Principal Davis's office at 9:00 PM."

"But it's not 9:00 PM," I said.

Maddie nodded. "Right. Like I said, once you're inside, it might make more sense."

"Should I worry about cameras and stuff?" I asked, putting my fingers on the handle of the door.

"Hope not," Maddie said, grinning as she handed me Linus's journal. "Take this with you."

Grabbing the leather notebook, I forced it into my back pocket. I shut my eyes and pushed the door open. Silently, I slipped into the office and let the door shut behind me. The light was switched off, but the room wasn't completely dark. I stepped across the carpet of the dead silent room, studying my surroundings.

In the entire time I've been at Buchanan, I had never once been to the principal's office, which was something I was quite proud of actually. The room was surprisingly larger than I thought it was going to be. A massive bookshelf stood against the wall at the back of the room. In front of that was the principal's desk, made entirely of wood. A leather chair was pushed into the desk.

The only light came from the computer monitor on Principal Davis's desk, but it was bright enough that I could easily see where I was walking.

Framed pictures hung on the wall next to me as I entered farther into the room. There was a small blinking red light at the ceiling. For a moment, I feared that there *was* a camera filming me until I saw that it was only a smoke detector.

The watch on my wrist chirped, and Maddie's voice spoke through the tiny speaker. "What do you see, Valentine?"

I studied the room again as I brought the watch up to my face. "There's a desk in the middle of the room, some pictures on the wall, and a huge bookshelf on the back wall."

"Do you see an eagle's nest anywhere?" she asked.

I looked at the bookshelf. "Nope," I replied. "I don't see a nest of any kind in here."

"Blasted!" her voice chirped. "Keep looking. What else do you see? Anything weird?"

I felt discouraged. "Nothing weird at all. It just looks like a boring office."

"9:00 PM," she said. "Maybe it's not referring to the time, but a direction. Face the principal's desk and look directly to your left."

"My left?" I asked.

"Yes, because if you were standing on a giant clock, 9 PM would be at your left."

Made sense, I thought. I faced the bookshelf and looked at the wall on my left, but it was the only wall that was completely empty. "Nothing," I said into my communicator.

I started walking to the bookshelf at the back of the room. The screen saver from the computer monitor

74

glowed against the books making them easy for me to read. I spoke softly to myself as I studied each shelf. "9:00 PM… eagle's nest at 9:00 PM."

The communicator chirped again. "What're you doing? Did you find anything yet?"

"No," I replied. "Nothing yet. I'm looking at his bookshelf though. Maybe there's something on here."

"Okay, but hurry up," Maddie said. "I think I hear someone coming."

At the top of the bookcase, I saw a green light pulsing on and off. Curious, I started climbing the shelves to get a better look. I only had to pull myself up about a foot before I could see what it was.

Sitting on the middle of the shelf was a round clock with a green dot in the center. Every couple seconds or so, it would slowly glow on and then fade away. Weird, I thought.

I looked at the numbers on the clock, and saw that it actually had the wrong time on it. The arms were pointed in such a way that it was permanently on 9 o'clock.

Clicking my watch again, I whispered. "Wait, I think I might've found something."

Maddie's voice didn't reply.

I clicked the watch again. "Maddie? You there? I said I think I might've found something!"

The only answer I received was the sound of static as it shushed through the tiny speaker. Was she in trouble? I'd have to be quick so I could get back to her.

I looked to the left of the clock, to where 9:00 PM

was pointing. Staring right at me was a thick book titled *Eagle's Nest.*

A chill traveled down my spine as I grabbed the book and hopped back to the floor. Before I opened it, I spoke into my communicator again. "Maddie, I found it! I found the Eagle's Nest! It's a *book!*"

Again, the communicator remained silent.

I wanted to run into the hallway to see if she was alright, but I was too excited about opening Linus's journal. I flipped the book upside-down and shook it back and forth. A miniature golden key bounced on the carpet.

Dropping to my knees, I laid the journal down in front of me. I pushed the key into the socket of the lock, and turned it carefully until I felt it click. Taking a breath, I flipped open the journal and looked inside.

It was empty.

I mean, there wasn't any writing inside it. Instead, the pages had been cut so that a small space was in the center of the book. Linus had turned the journal into a container, and in the middle of the container was a small video player. It was like one of those music players my dad uses when he goes for a run, but it also had a two-inch full color screen on the front of it, doubling as a video recorder.

"What in the world?" I whispered as I held the recorder in my hands. I clicked the "play" button, instantly booting up the device. Were all the passwords on this little video player?

The screen blinked and started playing whatever it was that Linus had been so keen on hiding. In the middle of the dark principal's office, I sat on the floor and watched silently.

It was a video taken a few weeks ago. The date at the beginning of the movie showed me that. It was dark and grainy, but I could tell it was filmed in the lower levers of Buchanan, the dungeon. The person doing the filming was also hidden from view because I could see they were behind a stack of boxes. Linus must've been the one to film it.

The video suddenly started to get shaky as two boys entered into the frame. I didn't recognize the boy on the right, but I knew who the boy on the left was immediately. It was the school president, Sebastian.

My eyes were glued to the screen as the two boys in the video started speaking.

"The box of goods is in the room back here," Sebastian said. "There's enough candy to last you at least a week this time."

The other boy looked nervous. "Here's the money from all the candy sales. Four hundred bucks total."

"Excellent. This is all going according to plan. You see? And you were worried this wasn't going to work."

"If you ask me now, I'd still say I was worried. How long do you think before the school finds out you're making money selling candy under the noses of the teachers?"

"Ha ha! They'll never find out! The teachers at this school have enough on their plate as it is. You think they really care that kids are eating candy? They're adults who are too distracted by their jobs. We're fine, and this *business is fine."*

"It's really brilliant of you to sell candy to sugar craving kids."

"What can I say? I see where money can be made, and I go there. Maybe you can learn a little somethin' from it."

"The students here don't even have a clue either. That's the best part."

"I know, right? They freely hand over their cash for a chocolate bar. It's unbelievable that they're willing to pay two bucks for a candy bar that cost me fifty cents. Morons."

"Alright then. You say the candy is in the backroom, sir?"

"Yep. I've got, like, ten boxes for you this time. Hand them out so your guys can sell them, but remember – only keep sales of this stuff in the dungeon. Taking it to the upper levels of Buchanan is too risky."

"Right. I'll get the new guy to help me out with the boxes."

"New guy? What new guy? You're supposed to clear all your little goons through me!"

"He's cool. His name is Linus. Trust me. He's legit."

"Hmmm, I don't know. I'll look into him. You'd better hope he's legit, or it's on you."

"Seriously, Sebastian, if Linus was an undercover agent, I'd know it."

"You dolt! I told you to never use my name!"

"Sorry, sir."

"You can never be too careful of who might be watching."

"Right."

"As always, I'll have another shipment of candy for you on Monday. Bring Linus with you. I'd like to meet this kid."

"You got it, sir."

The camera started to get shakier. Linus must've lost his balance because the screen became a blur of motion. Sebastian and the other boy noticed it instantly. I couldn't see their faces anymore, but their voices were still coming through clearly. My eyes felt strained from watching the camera shake wildly. Linus must've been running at this point because he sounded like a dog breathing heavily.

"Don't let him get away!" Sebastian's voice cried out.

"You there!" shouted the second boy's voice. *"Stop him! Get in front of him!"*

The camera shook one last time before the video cut out.

The knot in my stomach returned and my mouth suddenly felt dry. I felt like I was going to puke. This *was* worse than we thought. In fact, I found myself wishing it *was* about a set of stolen passwords. At least, that way it'd be easier to deal with.

I brought the wristwatch back to my face and spoke into the mic. "Maddie, we've got a serious problem here."

She still wasn't answering. Now I was worried.

Hopping to my feet, I slipped the video player into my front pocket and started running to the front door, but I didn't get very far.

At that moment, I felt a sharp pain at the back of my head, and then my entire world went black.

When I opened my eyes, I felt as if my head was spinning. I had no idea where I was except I knew I wasn't in Principal Davis's office anymore. The floor was cold, hard, and damp… and my socks were *wet*…

This brings us back to the beginning of the story, and now you're up to speed with all the junk I've gone through today. Everything that happened has brought me to this point – *not* my best day ever.

I heard the boy ask his question from the shadows of the room, but my head was swelling with pain. "What did you say?" I asked.

The boy paused and then repeated himself. "I *said*, you know this is *over*, right? This little game you and your friends are playing? They've already ratted you out, Brody. You're *done*."

It was a bluff – it *had* to be. Maddie wouldn't do that, would she? Then again, I'm not exactly friends with her so I'm not the expert in what she *would* and *wouldn't* do.

The boy continued to speak from the dark. "Y'know, we were actually getting a little worried that you weren't gonna wake up before the end of the school day. Someone even suggested that we bring the school nurse to see you."

I felt confused. "How long have I been out?"

The boy chuckled. "Almost the entire school day. It was second period when we picked you up, but now it's seventh period – only about twenty more minutes before school is dismissed."

The entire school day? They hit me hard enough to knock me out for almost *five hours?* To be fair though, I *am* a heavy sleeper, and despite the pain in my head, I actually felt well rested. "Where's Maddie?" I asked.

"Where's the *journal?*" the boy replied.

I shook my head and shut my eyes tight. "What're you even talking about? When you guys knocked me out, I was *looking* at the journal!"

The boy paused. "But if *that* was the journal…"

I lowered my gaze.

The boy spoke again. "The book you were looking at *was* the journal we're all after isn't it?"

I didn't answer.

"But it had a large hole cut out of it," he continued. "Which can only mean there was something *else* inside the journal. Something that you *found* before we grabbed you."

Glancing at my jeans, I could see the bump in my pocket from the video player I slipped into it. Whoever kidnapped me never bothered to check my pockets for anything! I could feel a fit of laughter coming on, but I pushed it down deep into my gut and tightened a smile. What a bunch of *noobs!*

The boy LOL'd. "You totally just gave yourself away, you know that?"

"What?" I asked, dazed.

"You *looked* at your pocket!" he said throwing his arms out. "You might as well have just *told* me it was in your jeans!"

I licked my teeth, trying to come up with a bluff of my own, but I still couldn't think straight. I guess *I* was the only noob in the room.

Finally, the boy stepped into the light, and I saw his

face clearly. It was Sebastian, the president of Buchanan School. He held his open palm to me. "Hand it over, Mr. Valentine."

Defeated, I reached into my pocket and removed the tiny video player. I set it into Sebastian's hand, but not without glaring at him the entire time. Man, if only I had laser eyes, right?

Just then, I heard the muffled sound of someone struggling nearby. I glanced over my shoulder, to the spot in the corner behind me. The whole area was shrouded in darkness, but there was definitely someone back there. It *had* to have been Maddie.

"Let her go!" I cried, facing Sebastian again.

Sebastian laughed. "You think that's *Madison* back there?"

Baffled, I said, "Well, I *did*... up until you said *that*."

I watched as the president stepped around my chair and to the other kid in the room. He grabbed both sides of their chair, and started dragging it across the floor. As he pulled it into the light, I saw that it actually *wasn't* Maddie. "Linus?" I whispered.

Linus leaned forward in the chair as the president released it. The tape over his mouth prevented him from talking, but it didn't stop him from groaning loudly. Sebastian pinched a corner of the tape and ripped it off Linus's face.

Linus clenched his teeth, sucking air through them, making the sound someone does when they get hurt.

"*Sssssssssssssssssssss!*"

I felt a wave of emotion splash through my body, and I started talking rapidly. "Where have you *been* all day? Did you *mean* to run into me this morning? Why did you decide to involve *me* in any of this? Have you been *planning* it for awhile?"

Linus took a breath and licked his lips. Then he glared at me. "I can't believe you just gave up my video player like that."

"*Why* can't you believe it?" I shouted, angry. "I'm just a kid that goes to school here that never asked for any of this! I didn't *want* this! I didn't wake up this morning thinking, 'hey, I hope I get caught up in some secret agent conspiracy today!'"

Linus shook his head at me disapprovingly. Then he looked at the president. "So now that you've got the video player, what do you intend on doing with it?"

"This thing?" the president asked as he held it up. "You can bet your little video will get deleted. None of what you've filmed will come to light."

"The truth will come out sooner or later," Linus replied as he exhaled slowly. He was pretty badly beaten up.

"But why?" I asked. "Why sell kids a bunch of candy? It doesn't make sense!"

"Doesn't it?" the president replied.

"Wait a second," I said, feeling confused. "Where's the list of passwords then? What happened to all that?"

Linus shook his head, staring at the ground. He spit on the cement and spoke. "There was never a list of passwords," he whispered. "I only said that to get Sebastian and his goons off my trail."

"It didn't work out that way, did it?" Sebastian growled.

"No," Linus whispered. "It didn't."

I still wasn't sure exactly what Sebastian was after. "So then… candy sales, and money? That's what you're doing? Because I'd be disappointed if your only goal in all this was to make money. That's a pretty stereotypical 'bad guy' thing to do. I would hope that after all the trouble I've been through today, you'd prove to be a *real* villain. Unless your evil plan is actually a *long term* one.

Are you going to be a dentist when you grow up? Are you giving everyone a crazy amount of cavities so they'll come see you one day?"

The president found my questions funny, and laughed an evil laugh. "Most of the times, it's the obvious answer that's correct. I'm sorry to disappoint you, but this *is* about money. I have no desire to grow up to become a super villain dentist."

"How unoriginal," I hissed.

The president set the video player on the table at the side of the room. "It might be unoriginal, but look who has the most power. Me. *I'm* the one making money off unsuspecting kids at this school, and you know the best part? They *willingly* give me their cash for candy bars. I control the candy sales, and you know what that means?"

Linus and I sat silently, waiting for Sebastian to answer his own question.

"It means *power*," the president finally said. "*Money* brings *power*."

"But you're the president of Buchanan," I said. "You've already *got* power."

Sebastian straightened his posture and adjusted his necktie. "It wasn't enough for me. As president, sure, I control a few things, but now that I have everyone's money, I'm on a whole new level of *control*."

"A whole new level of *crazy*," I said, under my breath.

"In the land of the poor, the richest kid is king," Sebastian said.

The way he said it made me cringe, and I was beginning to think he actually *did* sound like a real villain. To me, the difference between bad guys and villains is that bad guys *don't* consider themselves as bad guys because they *think* they're doing something *good*. Villains, on the other hand, *know* they're doing something *bad*, but don't care because they *want* to do it. President Sebastian was definitely starting to *sound* like a *villain*.

Sebastian tapped his hand on Linus's shoulder. "And you almost foiled my plans, didn't you?"

Linus jerked his shoulder away from the president's touch.

Sebastian continued. "And I can keep this up all year. My parents have a membership at one of those 'buy in bulk' stores so I have them pick up a few boxes every week. The teachers have no clue what's going on under them. It's hilarious actually."

I didn't see the humor in it. Burping the alphabet is hilarious – taking money from kids isn't. Great, I thought. Just what Buchanan needed – a bully with power. I wonder if adults ever had to deal with people like this.

All of a sudden, there was a short clicking sound on the cement floor. Sebastian spun in place and stared at the concrete, looking for the source of the noise. Linus and I also scanned the ground, but couldn't see anything.

And then the worst smell in the history of all smells entered my nose. It smelled like a sewage plant had exploded next to a graveyard of fish, and the fish just

finished having a dirty diaper fight, all in front of a pile
of burning tires.

It. Was. Awful.

STINK
LINES

Sebastian started hacking, as if he swallowed some
water down the wrong pipe. He clutched at his throat and
turned back to face us. "Which one of you let out that
fluffy biscuit?"

I stared at the president, completely puzzled by
what was just said.

"What's a *fluffy biscuit?*" Linus laughed.

Through his coughs, the president continued to
point blame at us. "You guys are sick, man! Sick! I can't
be in here! Oh man, I'm gonna *barf!*"

His reaction was hilarious, but I also felt like I was

about to puke all over the place. I looked at Linus, who had his hand up to me, telling me to wait a moment.

The president hacked again, and then sprinted toward the door. Without looking back, he flipped it open and jumped through. I could hear the pitter patter of his feet on linoleum as he darted down the hallway.

I pinched my nose shut and gasped for breath through my mouth. "What *is* that? OMG, it smells like my grandma's bathroom after we eat burritos!"

Linus jumped up from his chair and poked his head through the door. He stepped backward and snickered.

Maddie entered into the room with her hands over her mouth and nose. "Oh, that's awful!" she said, her voice muffled through her palms.

"What *is* it though?" I asked, embarrassed that my voice was a couple notches higher since I was pinching my nose shut.

"It's the stink bombs from the spy kit," Maddie said. "You stuffed them in your backpack, remember? But I've never used them before so I didn't know how many to set off... so I set *all* of them off."

My eyes were starting to water as I shuffled across the room. "At least it got Sebastian out of here, but he's still got the—" I shut my mouth, shocked as I looked at the table across the room. The video player was still there! I grabbed it and held it out to Maddie and Linus. "He forgot this! He left without taking it!"

Linus smiled. "We gotta get outta here before he comes back! And that'll be any second!"

"Yeah," Maddie said. "If it's not him, then you know he'll send some monitors our way."

"But what do we do with it?" Linus asked, stepping into the hallway. "School's almost out so we're running out of time! We need to show the student body this video, but *how*? How can we show *everybody* this video?"

And then I remembered the televisions Buchanan School had recently installed in the hallways. They were used to make announcements and were also hooked up to the school-wide speaker system. "We can use the televisions!"

Linus's jaw dropped as he slapped his thigh. "You're right! There has to be a way we can hook it up to those TVs! Where would the command center for that be though?"

"It has to be in the front office!" Maddie said. "I've made announcements a couple times, and every time I did, I had to speak into a little microphone in that office!"

"But do they play the videos there?" I asked.

"I don't know," said Linus, "but there's only one way to find out! Follow me!"

As Maddie and Linus sprinted down the hallway, I did my best to keep up with them, but that cramp in my side just wouldn't leave me alone. I slowed to a stop and rested my hands on my knees.

"Guys, wait!" I shouted.

Maddie stopped first. Linus ran a little more before he realized we weren't right behind him.

"What gives?" Maddie cried. "Are you alright?"

I nodded as I approached her. "Yeah, I'm fine," I said, holding the small video player out to her. "Take this though. I'm done. I just can't do this anymore."

Maddie's look of concern morphed into a look of anger. "What do mean? You've been doing this all day and you wanna quit right before the finish line?"

I sighed, nodding. "I'm not like you guys. I'm not cool or popular or sporty or whatever… it's probably best if you two take off without me. I'm only holding you back."

"Right," Linus said, upset. "Because we're waiting around for you to make a decision right now!"

"I thought I could do this," I said. "But it turns out I can't. I just can't run around pretending to be something I'm not."

Maddie walked toward me. I could tell from the tone of her voice that she was still angry. "Let me tell you the truth about life – nobody is ever what they *pretend* to be. You probably look at all the cool kids and think they've got their stuff together, but they don't. They're exactly like you, but with one important difference – they know who they *want* to be, and they're working toward that goal. If you don't have something you're reaching for, then life is *safe* isn't it? And safe is *boring*."

I curled my lip and shook my head. It was like she could read my mind! Easy is boring, and boring is good... *used* to be good. The truth was that this entire day came out of left field... but I wouldn't have wanted it any other way.

Linus put his hand on my shoulder. "You were a secret agent with Maddie today, right?"

I nodded. "I was a kid helping a friend."

"Then *that's* who you are," Maddie said with a smirk.

Out of the blue, I heard Colton's voice speak sharply. "Isn't this cute. It looks like the three of you are dishin' out life lessons over here. Care to spoon a couple dollops into a bowl for me?"

At the corner of the hallway, I saw Colton and his two hall monitors blocking our path. The president was behind them, plugging his nose, and yelling with a high-pitched voice. "Get them! They've got something that belongs to me!"

Linus spun in place. He grabbed Maddie's hand and looked back at me. Then he moved his other hand toward my body and pretended to snatch the video player. With a smile, he winked at me, and I knew exactly what he was thinking. He wanted to act as if he had the video player in his hands so the monitors would chase after him instead of me. Pulling Maddie down the hallway, Linus started running toward Colton and the president.

Immediately, I took off in the opposite direction. I heard the president shouting from behind me and when I looked back, I saw the monitors chasing after Maddie and Linus. Their plan had worked!

I could feel the tiny rectangular video player in my hand as I neared the end of the corridor. The halls of Buchanan were designed almost like a flower, with the front lobby being at the center. All passages hooked long circles until meeting back at the center, which meant that if you followed your path long enough, you'd find yourself in the front lobby.

Maddie and Linus had run in one direction, and I was sprinting down the opposite path they took, but eventually our paths would cross again. I only hoped that they'd be smart enough to guide the monitors down another part of the school, and away from the front office. Of course they would... secret agents are smart like that.

My shoes squeaked on the freshly polished linoleum flooring as I bolted through the halls of Buchanan. The green lockers on both sides of me became a blur the faster I ran. In the entire time I've been a student here, I've never torn through a hallway like this – it was *exciting*. Without any teachers to order me to slow down, I felt as free as a bird. My side wasn't even cramping!

As the corner bent a little more sharply, I was forced to slow down, which gave me enough time to see if any of the monitors were following me. I was relieved to see they *weren't*.

There wasn't much time left before school let out. I only had minutes at most, so whatever was going to happen needed to happen fast. With the video player in my hand, it was my responsibility to get to the front offices and figure out how to get it to broadcast over the school's television sets.

Without Maddie or Linus to help guide me, I was totally on my own, and you know what? I *loved* it. For the first time in the entire day, I actually felt like *I* was in control of the situation. Buchanan's president was at the heart of a major scandal, and it was up to me to let everyone know about it.

Finally, the front lobby came into view as I took the last turn in the hall. I burst into the area and headed for the office. Pressing the handle down, I heard a click and pushed the door open. The motions lights flickered on overhead, which meant there wasn't anyone else in there. Good thing too because if there was, I'm not sure what I would've done.

There was a long rectangular counter that separated the front of the office from the back. I could see several computer monitors glowing, but no obvious place for me to hook up the video player. Sitting at the end of the counter was an old rusted microphone. I remembered that Maddie said she made the announcements through that a few times, so I knew I had to be close.

I pulled myself up on the counter and swung my legs around until landing on my feet on the other side. I heard my shirt tear and felt a pain as something scraped my arm. Along the side of the counter were plastic hooks that stuck out a few inches. Hanging from those hooks were sets of keys, probably for doors in the school. "Great," I muttered as I examined my torn sleeve. "Mom's not gonna be happy with *that*."

I turned around, and then I saw it – the area *under* the microphone had a small box hooked up to several kinds of video machines. There was a laptop computer, a DVD player, a CD player, and a cable that was hanging freely. It was the same kind of cable my dad used to hook our digital camera up to our television at home. That was it!

But before I could do anything, someone punched me right in my back. I keeled over against the counter, luckily missing all the hooks. Groaning in pain, I rolled to my back and saw Colton standing over me. "You punched me in the *back!*"

ANGRY COLTON

"You've become a real *thorn* in my side, you know that?" Colton growled.

I chuckled, scooting myself backward. "The school *deserves* to know the truth… the truth the president desperately wants to *hide!* These kids are getting taken advantage of by a bully in a suit, and I'm gonna make sure it doesn't happen again!"

Colton stepped forward. "Hand over the device!"

Holding my side, I scooted across the carpet, away from the crazy kid. "How can you take orders from Sebastian?" I shouted. "How can you choose to be on his team after all he's done?"

Colton wiped his lip as he stepped toward me. "I don't know anything about what you're talking about. All I know is that the school's president gave me the order to get that thing back from you, so that's what I'm doing!"

"So you don't even know what's on here?" I asked.

Colton shook his head. "It's none of my business, and by the bad day you've had, I'd say it was none of *yours* either."

Holding the video player in my fist, I kept inching my way closer to the hanging cable under the mic. "You're making a mistake," I said, noticing that Colton was next to the plastic hooks.

Colton's face clenched up as he grew angrier. "I'm afraid you're the one who's made a mistake!" he cried as he reached for me.

I dropped the video player and rolled to my feet. Just as I stood, Colton grabbed my shirt and squeezed his fists tight. I held his wrists as he pushed me backward, but I caught the counter with my foot and shoved back.

We struggled against each other until I finally managed to get my arms between us. With all of my might, I pushed against him, separating us completely. Colton fell against the counter, losing his balance. With my free hand, I grabbed the back of his leather belt and forced him back until I felt the exposed hooks. With the rest of my strength, I lifted him up until his belt was over one of the plastic hooks, and then I let go.

"Hey!" Colton shouted. *"What're you doing?"*

I caught my breath as I stumbled about. *"Hang out* and you'll see," I sneered in my best "action hero" voice.

Colton was half a foot off the ground, kicking his feet wildly. He was high enough that he couldn't touch the floor.

I turned around, and limped over to the video player. There were only a few minutes of class remaining so I had time. After I grabbed device from the floor, I connected the hanging cable into the socket at the top. The televisions in the hallway flashed on instantly. Shutting my eyes, I hit the play button. The speakers in the ceiling rasped as the sound of President Sebastian's voice spoke. Through the windows of the front office, I watched the footage all over again as it played through every TV in the school.

Colton's jaw dropped as he stared at the video feed. "I'll be a monkey's uncle…" he whispered.

The cafeteria was right across the lobby and through the windows, I could see kids raise their heads as the footage played on. Their faces were shocked as the president spoke on over the speakers.

Linus and Maddie suddenly appeared in the lobby. The hall monitors chasing after them slowed to a stop in front of the television and all four of them watched. Maddie hadn't seen the video yet, so she cupped her hand over her mouth, stunned.

Sebastian appeared jogging through the lobby and clutching at his side, probably from a cramp. His eyes were peeled wide open as he gawked at the television screen. I couldn't hear his voice, but I could read his lips as he said, "No no no no no…"

When the video finally finished, the television screens blinked, and switched off. It was done at last, and the weight on my shoulders disappeared.

For the last time, the speaker in the ceiling cackled. "President Sebastian, please report to the principal's office. Sebastian, please report to the principal's office. *NOW!*"

Through the window, I saw Sebastian glare at me. I was almost afraid that his eyes were going to crack the glass. The two hall monitors took him by the arms and marched him down the lobby, disappearing through the door to Principal Davis's office.

Maddie and Linus stepped into the room I was in. Maddie had a grin beaming on her face as Linus helped Colton off the hook on the counter.

"We're not going to have any more trouble, are we?" Linus asked the boy hanging from the plastic hook.

Colton sighed as the tension vanished from his face. "Nope. As far as I see it, this is over. I'm pretty sure my orders won't be coming from Sebastian anytime soon."

"What'll you do now?" Linus asked Colton.

Colton shrugged his shoulders. "I'm not sure," he said. "I think after all this, I'll need a vacation."

Maddie and Linus laughed. Colton nodded his head at me, and stepped out of the room.

Linus turned and spoke. "Looks like you saved the day, rookie."

"I couldn't have done it without you two," I replied, winking at Maddie. "But what about the principal? We still don't know if he's in on it."

Linus shook his head. "He's *not*. My orders came from *him*. They always do. He knew something was going on with the candy sales and ordered me to go undercover and look into it."

"But why was the journal hidden in his office then?" Maddie asked.

"Because Sebastian was already coming after me, and I figured that's the last place he would ever think to look," Linus replied. "I mean, who's crazy enough to break into Principal Davis's office?"

Maddie pointed her thumb at me. "*This* guy."

"You really proved yourself to be somethin' else today, Mr. Valentine," Linus said, putting a hand on my shoulder. "We could really use a kid like you on our team."

"You mean you didn't choose me on purpose?" I asked.

Linus laughed. "No, I *did* choose you. I've been thinking you'd be a good addition for some time now. I'm just glad it wasn't a mistake."

"But we never did anything together that would get you to think that," I replied.

"I could just see it in you," Linus said confidently.

"Sometimes it takes that extra little push to get people to do great things," Maddie added.

I scratched the back of my neck and took a deep breath. "I still think this might've been a little *too* much excitement for one day."

Maddie threw her arms out. "Oh, come on, Brody! You know this was probably the best day you've ever had!"

I stood thinking for a moment – now that I know there's a secret agency working in the shadows of Buchanan School, I'm not sure I could go on living the life of a normal student ever again.

Another smile appeared on Maddie's face. "The life of an agent is never dull."

"She's right," Linus added. "Sebastian's scandal with the candy was just the *tip* of the iceberg. There's more going on than anyone knows."

Now I was curious. "Like what?"

Maddie wagged her finger at me as she stepped toward the door. "That's classified information that only *agents* are allowed to know…"

Linus set a business card down on the counter. The only thing printed on it was an inkblot in the shape of a raven and some roman numerals. "If you're interested in what we're offering… you can find us there," he said, walking behind Maddie out of the room.

I stared at the business card – a raven with some roman numerals underneath it. It was obvious that the picture of the raven was a clue I had to solve in order to find the agency Linus and Maddie were a part of. I couldn't help but smirk at the idea of having to figure it out.

The bell to the school rang as I approached the exit to the office. As kids raced through the lobby, I could hear fits of laughter echo off the walls as they gossiped about Sebastian and the video they just watched.

It occurred to me that it wasn't so much the sugary treats that were a bad thing, but the idea that someone was ripping kids off by selling those treats in an underground market. The vending machines with healthy snacks weren't going anywhere anytime soon, but maybe Principal Davis would be open to the idea of having a few junkie items. I mean, the majority of students at Buchanan School *were* kids, right?

Leaning in the entryway to the front office, I tried to see where Maddie and Linus might've gone, but amidst the sea of students, they had completely vanished. I overheard some of the others laughing, joking about Sebastian's scandal, and how this was probably the most awful day Buchanan School had ever seen.

A smile broke on my face as Maddie's words slipped into my mind again. I glanced at the business card, and realized she was absolutely correct. While this might've been a bad day for Buchanan School, it definitely turned out to be one of the *best* days in *my* life.

I watched the faces of kids as they passed me, and then remembered the other thing Maddie had said. Nobody had their act together any more than I did.

But the difference between then and now was that now I *knew* who I wanted to be now, and I knew what I had to do to get there.

Shutting my eyes, I stepped out of the room as Brody Valentine, and into the hall as *secret agent* Brody Valentine. I was determined to do everything I could to find the answer to Linus's business card, and become the agent I was *born* to be.

...let's just hope there aren't any *bees* involved.

Stories – what an incredible way to open one's mind to a fantastic world of adventure. It's my hope that this story has inspired you in some way, lighting a fire that maybe you didn't know you had. Keep that flame burning no matter what. It represents your sense of adventure and creativity, and that's something nobody can take from you. Thanks for reading! If you enjoyed this book, I ask that you help spread the word by sharing it or leaving an honest review!

- Marcus
m@MarcusEmerson.com

Oh, the life of being a ninja. I know what you're thinking – it's an awesome life filled with secrets, crazy ninja moves, and running on the tops of trees. Well, you're right. I'm not gonna lie to you – it's an absolutely *fantastic* life.

But it wasn't always that way.

This might surprise you, but ninjas are often seen as the *bad* guys. I know, right? I had no idea either until I became one. Though looking back, I should've seen the signs early on. You know what they say – hindsight is 20/20.

So this is my story – my diary…er, my *chronicle*. I feel as though it has to be told for others to read so they can learn about the events at Buchanan School. History has to be studied and learned from or else it's destined to repeat itself. And that's something I cannot allow.

My name is Chase Cooper, and I'm eleven years old.

I'm the kind of kid that likes to read comic books and watch old horror movies with my dad. If you were to see me walking down the street, you'd try your best not to bump into me, but only because I'm sorta scrawny. I see all these articles online with titles about losing weight and getting rid of unwanted body fat, and my jaw just drops because I can't gain weight to save my life! I've started working out with my dad when he gets home from work, but it's hard to keep up with him.

All this to say that if you saw me, the last thing you'd think was "dangerous ninja."

I'm not the most popular kid in school, that's for sure. I've never had a girlfriend, and I've never played sports outside of gym class. That's not true – I was on a soccer team in third grade, but after a shin guard to the face and a broken nose, I quit.

So I'm scrawny and unpopular. What else can I apply to those two traits for a completely wretched experience? The *start* of school. But wait! Let's multiply that by a million – I'm also the *new* kid at this particular school.

My parents decided to move across town over the summer so we could live in a slightly larger house. I mean, really? How selfish is *that*? A bigger house, but social death for me! Being in a new district means an entire herd of new students that I don't know.

Well, that's not entirely true either. I know Zoe. She's the same age as me, but doesn't really count because she's my cousin.

Luckily, we had the same gym class together. She was surprised to see me on that first day. I remember it well – it was a Monday, and the day I caught my first glimpse of the ninjas at Buchanan.

"Chase?" Zoe asked. She was wearing gym shorts and a tank top with the school's mascot on it.

"Hey, Zoe," I said.

She looked surprised. "It *is* you! What're you doing *here*?"

Going to school, dummy. That's what I *wanted* to say, but decided against it. "My parents moved to this side of town so I go to school here now."

Zoe laughed. "That's so cool! My own cousin in the same school as me! What fun we'll have!"

I looked at her silky hair and perfect skin. She kind of looked like one of those models on teenybopper magazines. Yeah, there was no way she'd keep herself affiliated with the likes of me, but I gave her the benefit of the doubt. "Uh-huh, it'll be great," I sighed.

The coach, Mr. Cooper, was at the front of the gymnasium checking off students he knew. He walked up to the rest and asked for their names and grade. Finally, he approached Zoe and me.

"Good morning, Zoe," Mr. Cooper said as he scraped a checkmark into the attendance list. Then he looked at me. "And what's your name?"

Zoe answered for me. "This is Chase Cooper. He's my cousin," she said with a smile.

"Good to have you here," said Mr. Cooper. Then he pointed at Zoe. "She's a good kid to have as a cousin. It's the start of school, but I've already seen her on several try-out lists. You'll do good to follow her lead."

I faked a smile. "Sure."

As Mr. Cooper walked away, Zoe continued speaking. "Why didn't you tell me you were starting at this school?"

I shrugged my shoulders. "We don't really talk that much, and it never came up in conversation. We hardly ever see each other."

Zoe crinkled her nose. "We see each other *every weekend*. Our families have Sunday brunch together at the park!"

I couldn't argue with her. "It's just a little embarrassing."

"You have nothing to be embarrassed about. Starting a new school might be weird, but it's not like you have the ability to control a situation like that," she said.

I didn't want to tell her I was embarrassed and scared of being the new kid. That making friends isn't a strength of mine, and I'm destined to be that kid who walks swiftly through the hallways, clutching my backpack straps and staring at the floor, hoping I don't make eye contact with someone with anger management issues. So I didn't say any of that. "You're right. I think it's just the first day jitters, y'know?"

Zoe's eyes sparkled. She didn't have a clue. "Welcome to the club. We've *all* got the first day jitters. My dad always says the pool is coldest when you first touch the water so the best thing to do is dive right in."

I wasn't sure what my cousin was trying to say. So I replied with, "Wise words."

Zoe looked off to her left and noticed a boy standing alone. "That's Wyatt. He's never really talked to anyone here. He keeps to himself – always has. Which is why he probably doesn't have any friends."

Wyatt was short. He had wavy black hair and a pale complexion that would make a vampire jealous. He kind of looked like a porcelain doll. "Has anyone tried to be *his* friend?"

"Actually, yes. *I* tried talking to him last year, but he wouldn't hear any of it," she sighed. "He was a *jerk* to me."

"Why are you telling me this?" I asked.

Zoe glanced at me. "Because I don't want you to be like him."

I tightened a smile. When I looked back at Wyatt, he was gone.

"So have you raised any money yet for the food drive?" Zoe asked out of nowhere.

"Food drive?" I asked. "I haven't heard of anything about that."

"They sent a pamphlet to all of the student's houses last week," she said. "Oh, that's right... you just moved into your new place, didn't you?"

I nodded.

"Well, it's probably somewhere at your house. We're supposed to raise money by selling fruit or something. I'm already up to ten boxes sold."

"Is there a prize or anything?" I asked. Normally these kinds of things had cool prizes – ray guns and little helicopters and stuff.

"Not a prize for one person, but if the school collectively raises over ten grand, we get to take a trip the week before school is out."

"Where to?"

Zoe shrugged her shoulders. "Does it matter? Anything to get out of school for a day."

I smiled at my cousin. She was actually a little cooler than I thought.

Mr. Cooper opened the side door to the gymnasium. Thank goodness too because Zoe's conversation was making me feel a little edgy. He stepped outside and held the door open with his foot, ushering the rest of us to exit the gym for some "productive activity" outside. Great, just what I needed. Exercise.

Marcus Emerson is the author of several highly imaginative children's books including the 6th Grade Ninja series, Secret Agent 6th Grader, Lunchroom Wars, and the Adventure Club Series. His goal is to create children's books that are engaging, funny, and inspirational for kids of all ages - even the adults who secretly never grew up.

Born and raised in Colorado Springs, Marcus Emerson is currently having the time of his life with his beautiful wife Anna and their three amazing children. He still dreams of becoming an astronaut someday and walking on Mars.

Made in the USA
Lexington, KY
23 September 2014